Also by Cassandra Rose Clarke

The Magic of Blood and Sea

The Magic of Wind and Mist

The Mad Scientist's Daughter

The Witch Who Came in from the Cold

Our Lady of the Ice

Star's End

Halo: Battle Born

THE MANTICORE'S VOW

Cover illustration by Maria Anismova

Edited by Holly Lyn Walrath

Published by Interstellar Flight Press, Houston, Texas.

www.interstellarflightpress.com

ISBN (eBook): 978-1-7338862-2-2

ISBN (paperback): 978-1-7338862-0-8

ISBN (hardback): 978-1-7338862-1-5

First Edition: June 2019

THE MANTICORE'S VOW

And Other Stories

CASSANDRA ROSE CLARKE

INTERSTELLAR FLIGHT PRESS

The Manticore's Vow

I waited beneath the cover of an acacia tree for Zhepheren to arrive. We had agreed to meet when the Star of Lishinni rose, and it glowed now, its bluish tint more brilliant than the light of any of the other stars.

"Where is he, servant-human?" I hissed.

"I do not know." My servant-human shifted her weight as though nervous. She was called Ami by the other humans, and although it wasn't proper, I thought of her as Ami in my head. "I can run to his nest to check—" Her voice wobbled, and I caught the sweet tang of human fear. She did not want to go to Zhepheren's nest.

"That won't be necessary." I paced around the base of the acacia tree, flicking my tail back and forth. "I can go myself, if need be." I stopped and squinted off on the horizon. A figure slunk through the moonlight, long and lean, his pale mane glowing. "Zhepheren!" I cried, forgetting myself.

"My lady manticore should be quiet," Ami whispered. "The guards may hear."

I ignored her and bolted over the sand. Zhepheren trotted toward me. "Hello, Ongraygeeomryn," he said. "Are you ready for our journey?" He paused, one paw lifted off the ground. "Did you bring your *servant?*"

"Of course." I turned back to the acacia tree. Ami's head was tilted down, but I could tell that she watched us through the tangled web of her hair. "I needed someone to carry our supplies."

Zhepheren snorted. "I won't carry her if she can't keep up."

"She can keep up." We walked side by side, back to the tree. Ami lifted the supply bag and slung it over her shoulder.

"Are you ready, my lord, my lady?" She bowed a little, as if the weight of the supply bag were too much for her.

Zhepheren nodded. "We need to follow the Lishinni's light as far as we can before sunrise."

I didn't mention that he was the one who'd been late, that I'd been waiting for him since the star was a tiny dot just above the horizon line.

"What will we do come sunrise?" I asked, quivering with excitement. Ami gave me a tired look.

"Make camp and sleep through the day's heat." Zhepheren shook out his mane with an air of authority. He'd made this trip before, crossing the red wastes to reach the Oasis that housed the magic necessary to send us across the plains of water, into the human world. I believed him, of course, because he was the son of Ashnystion, and everyone knew that Ashnystion had traveled the human lands of the east. The musicians sang stories of him at royal dinners. It was quite exciting, having Ashnystion's son as a friend, and especially so since I'd learned that my parents didn't approve.

We set out on our journey without any of the fanfare of songs, only a jerk of Zhepheren's head toward the open waste. Our paws padded softly against the sand, and Ami trailed behind us, silent in the way only humans can be. The night was cool and dry against my fur, and it smelled of the wastes, of sand and salt and distant water. And occasionally it smelled of Zhepheren.

"Are you excited to travel the human lands?" I asked him when I couldn't stand the silence any longer. "Where do you think the Oasis will take us?"

"It'll take us where it wants to take us," Zhepheren said, sounding like the fortune-teller in my father's employ. "You cannot dictate to it. But I suppose it'll be interesting."

"Interesting!" I cried. "It'll be more than interesting. The humans are no match for us. We'll be rulers of their kingdoms in only a few days' time."

Zhepheren looked at me sideways, beneath the billowing cloud of his mane. "You're the daughter of rulers here. Which means you'll be ruler proper in time."

"Yes, but of *manticores*. I want to be a ruler of humans."

"You rule the servants."

"That's not the same!" I shook my head. "You understand nothing."

He trumpeted, trilling and amused. "I understand how to get you to the human lands, my princess."

I trotted up ahead of him, not wanting to listen to his insolence any longer. "Servant-human!" I barked, and Ami joined me at my side, pushing her hair out of her eyes. "Entertain me," I said.

"How would you like to be entertained, my lady?"

"With a story." I paused, thinking. "A human story. So I can know how your kind thinks, when I'm their ruler."

Ami nodded. She walked along beside me for a moment before speaking. "There once was a girl who lived in a village in the desert. She was very plain, and she longed to be beautiful. One day a traveling wizard came to see her. 'Can you make me beautiful?' she asked him, and he said yes. He gave her a tea to brew and drink, once a day for five days. She did exactly as he asked. On the fifth day, she transformed into a rose bush, with bright red blooms that never died. People traveled from all over the world to marvel at the beauty of the desert rose bush."

The wind rippled over us, stirring up clouds of sand.

"Is that it?" I asked.

Ami nodded. "Did it please you, my lady?"

"I don't understand it." I flapped my wings once in frustration. "Are all human stories like this?"

Ami gave a little squeak of fear and said, "Yes, my lady. My mother told me that when I was a child. She said it did no good to wish for things you can't have, and that using magic to make things as you like is dangerous."

At that last part of her explanation, I stopped and stared at her. She cowered back, her eyes on the ground.

"I will make an excellent leader of humans," I said. "Don't question my ability to work magic."

"Yes, my lady. I'm sorry, my lady, it wasn't my place—" She crouched down in the sand, her head bowed lowed, seeking recrimination. Zhepheren trotted past us and kicked up red dirt.

"We need to hurry," he said.

"Stand up," I told Ami. "But no more stories." I never cared for punishing my servants. My father told me it was necessary, and that I'd need to learn to do it when I was queen. But as ruler of the humans, I'd delegate such work to others.

"Hurry!" Zhepheren shouted into the blustering wind. I nudged at Ami to draw her to her feet, and we continued on our way, Ami murmuring apologies as we walked. I acknowledged them with a flick of my tail, and Ami told no more stories on our journey.

WE TRAVELED for two more days, journeying during the cool nights and sleeping beneath the sweltering sun. Every morning Zhepheren and I would loll in the sand, resting, as Ami set up our tent. She worked quickly and we were always tucked under the shade by the time the sun rose. I allowed her to sleep at my side, rather than out in the sun, because humans are much weaker than manticores, and I did not want her to fall ill.

It was a much more exhausting journey than I had expected. In songs, the details of journeys such as ours are always glossed over in favor of the glory of the arrival, which results in magic or battle or both. I had taken this to mean that the journeys were easy and thus not worth talking about. In truth, my limbs ached at the end of every night, and although Ami would rub her hands into my muscles, it did little to relieve the pain. We rationed the water so that we would not run out, and Zhepheren and I hunted the snakes that twisted sideways through the red sand. They proved a most unsatisfying meal.

On the third night, I began to regret my decision to accompany Zhepheren to the Oasis. As princess of the pride, I could have demanded him to bring the Oasis' magic to me, where I would cast the spell from the comfort of the royal garden, surrounded by soft fluttering flowers. But I wanted the adventure. Being princess of the pride is so *dull*.

Besides, my parents would never have approved of my plan to invade the human world. They were narrow-sighted, like most noble manticores. Zhepheren had accused me of being narrow-sighted once, but I doubted that he saw me as narrow-sighted now.

On and on we walked. The red sand was dark in the moonlight, like old blood. Ami shuffled along beside me, her shoulders slumped from the weight of our pack. We had not been walking long, and I was already growing weary. But then Zhepheren said:

"There!"

All three of us stopped in place. Ami lifted her head, her eyes wide and bright in the darkness. Zhepheren pointed with one paw. At first I saw nothing but the night's shadows, but then, slowly, forms began to emerge out of the moonlight. They were tall and thin and waved back and forth in the wind.

"Is that the Oasis?" I whispered.

"I told you I knew the way." Zhepheren flapped his wings once in a show of pride. "Come, we'll work the magic together."

He trotted forward, his mane shining like starlight. I followed him, but after a few paces I noticed that Ami hung back.

"Servant-human! Join me at once."

She hesitated. I didn't like this. The servant-humans were not supposed to hesitate.

"Now!" I cried.

Up ahead, Zhepheren had stopped. I could feel him staring at me, and my wings flushed with embarrassment.

"Do as I say, servant-human!"

Ami crept forward. As she drew close to me I saw that she was shaking.

"I'm sorry, my lady." She looked down at the sand. "But don't you feel it? This place—this place isn't right."

She peered up at me. Her face was streaked with red sand, and her hair was mattered against the side of her head.

"I don't feel anything," I said. "But it's the Oasis! It's why we journeyed across the wastes." I tilted my head toward the shapes in the darkness. "Come. When we've overthrown the human rulers, I'll give you your freedom and a concubine to keep you company."

"My freedom, my lady?" She blinked at me. "Is that possible?"

It wasn't, under manticore law, but I would make my own laws as ruler of the humans. "Of course. Come along."

But still she hesitated. The fear rose off of her like perfume, strong and pungent. She stepped backward, shaking her head.

"What is it?" I snapped. "What are you scared of?"

"It's *wrong*," she said, as if that offered any explanation. "It doesn't feel right."

"Why are you taking so long?" Zhepheren's voice rang out over the desert. "We've only a narrow opportunity to work the magic. Hurry!"

"Did you hear that?" I said to Ami. "A narrow opportunity. Stop being so human and come along."

Ami sagged her head, looking defeated. But when I walked toward the Oasis she followed, the scent of her fear floating along with her. Zhepheren wrinkled his nose when we passed.

"I told you that you shouldn't have brought her," he said.

"Hush!"

We walked in a line toward the dark shapes. As we approached, I saw that they were trees of a sort, although not like any tree I had ever seen. Their trunks were very narrow, and their leaves splayed out like the tail feathers of the great blue birds my father kept for sport. The wind gusted through the trees, knocking them together. Their scent was peculiar, like the soil and the north wind combined.

Ami whimpered beside me, whispering silly human incantations against evil magic.

"There's nothing to be afraid of!" I told her. "Zhepheren's father has come before."

Zhepheren nodded, sticking out his chest.

We came to the edge of the Oasis. The wind was stronger here, and cold, much colder than any wind I'd ever felt before. The moonlight shone through the trees, catching on those strange feathery leaves and casting broken patterns across the sand.

"Now what do we do?" I asked Zhepheren.

"We find the Artifact." He spoke this with the grave wisdom of a scholar, and I could hear that the word *artifact* was important, a name unto itself. "It's located in the center of the Oasis."

I didn't move. Although I had traveled all this way, the idea of crossing the line between sand and tree unsettled me. Stupid Ami! Her human fear had corrupted my thoughts.

"We'll have to do it tonight," Zhepheren said. "When the moon is full."

Curses! I knew that too, of course; it was the entire reason we had chosen these few days to travel. I took a deep breath.

"Are you ready, my princess?" Zhepheren asked in a sly voice.

"Of course I'm ready!" I looked to Ami. "Servant-human, accompany me."

She gave me a hollow, mournful look, but she didn't protest. Together, Ami and I walked into the trees, and Zhepheren followed. Ami gasped when we left the sand, and her hand knotted into my mane. I did not reprimand her, because I was frightened as well. The air was different here, thicker and colder. It burned in my lungs and seemed to shimmer just out of my line of sight, like a heat mirage. Ami's whispered incantations grew more urgent.

We crept forward. The ground underneath felt odd against my feet, spongy and damp, like I could sink through the soil. The trees rustled around us, gusting with the wind. They seemed to be speaking, but I could not understand what they said.

"This way." Zhepheren pointed with the tip of his tail. We veered to the left, but the path looked the same as it had before.

"Are you sure this is the right way?" I asked.

Zhepheren turned to me, scowling, and I immediately went hot with embarrassment. I didn't want him to think badly of me.

"Of course I'm sure," he said. "Look at the pattern in the moonlight. It marks the way."

I looked down to the ground, at the shards of silver light sliding back and forth with the wind. I didn't see it at first. Then Ami yelped, and her grip on my fur tightened. The jumbled pattern of moonlight reformed as I was watching, the path flickering with the movement of the trees. The shadows formed a path out of the light.

"Oh," I said.

Zhepheren flicked his tail and said, "You should learn to trust me, my princess."

"I do trust you!" Now that I had found the path it was all I could see. "I was just frightened, is all." In truth I'd thought he might have made a mistake, but I didn't think Zhepheren would like hearing that.

We walked for some time, longer than I thought we should. From the desert, the Oasis had seemed small, a speck of green against the red wastes. But now that we were inside the trees, it seemed to stretch on forever.

Then the path brightened.

"Oh!" I said. "Something's changed."

"We're almost there." Zhepheren surged forward, almost galloping, his wings and tail lifted high above his body. Ami pressed close to me.

"It's all right," I told her. "It's my responsibility to care for you. Father would be very upset if you died."

"If I may, my lady," she whispered. "I don't like this. It seems unnatural, even for magic."

I shushed her, even though part of me agreed. Zhepheren disappeared around a bend in the path, and I panicked, afraid the trees had swallowed him whole. But then he let out a great, triumphant trumpet, loud enough that the trees shook.

"He found it!" I cried, and I ran forward too, forgetting Ami and my fear both in my excitement. The path twisted around and revealed a clearing in the trees. It was flooded with moonlight, bright enough you could mistake it for day.

Tall pale grasses rippled in the wind, and at the center of the clearing rose a statue of a human.

I stopped on the clearing's edge. Zhepheren had trampled a path through the grass, although I noticed he had not stepped terribly close to the statue. It was a grotesque thing, the human form sinewy and thin. The figure did not have a face, only a blank oval surrounded by a swirl of flat human hair.

The statue glowed in the moonlight, eerie and unnatural.

"Zhepheren?" I called out uncertainly.

He turned to me. He didn't look like himself in the silver light.

"Here it is, my princess. As promised. The Artifact."

I crept forward into the clearing. The air felt different once I left the trees, thick and sweet like desert wine. I could feel the moonlight on my fur.

Zhepheren waited for me beside the statue. I joined him and we both looked up at it, gleaming in the light. I realized I could no longer smell Ami, but when I turned to the woods I saw her hanging back in the shadows, her eyes wide. My senses were muted. I couldn't smell her or hear her feet moving over the pine needles.

"Are you sure it's safe?" I asked Zhepheren.

"It's magic." He was still staring up at the statue, his face enraptured.

I did not understand his answer. I didn't have much experience with magic.

"Now what do we do?" I asked.

"We activate the Artifact, and it will whirl us away to the human lands." Zhepheren trotted in a circle around the statue and then sat back on his haunches. He never once looked away from it.

"And how do we activate it?" I asked.

Zhepheren flapped his wings once and didn't answer.

"Zhepheren?"

He trumpeted in frustration. "I do not know, my princess! The songs always passed over that part."

I glared at him. "You learned all this from the *songs?*"

"No. I learned the way from my father. But he never told me how to activate the magic." Zhepheren stood up and propped his two front paws on the statue's base. It stared blindly out in the thick moonlight.

Fool! Zhepheren knew as much as I did about the Oasis' magic. I trotted over to the edge of the woods, where Ami cowered in the shadows.

"Are you ready to leave, my lady?" she asked, and despite my dampened senses I heard the hopefulness in her voice.

"No!" I arched my tail. "Sing the ballad of Ashnystion."

She stared at me, trembling. Then she took a deep breath and began to sing. It was a familiar tale, one that's often shared at royal feasts. Ashnystion travels far and wide across the red wastes, to an oasis beneath the Star of Lishinni. He discovers magic there—magic in stone, the song goes, magic full of light. Magic brought forth by the sound of his voice.

And then he's whisked away to the human lands.

"Stop!" I commanded Ami. Her voice fell away. "That's all there is? No longer version?"

"That's the version we always perform for you."

Magic in stone, magic full of light, magic brought forth by the sound of his voice. The first two items made sense, of course, but the third—Zhepheren and I had both spoken in the presence of the statue, but it had accomplished nothing.

"Perhaps we should just leave," Ami said, but I ignored her, turning from the trees and stepping back out into the clearing. Zhepheren was still gazing up at the statue.

"The ballad says it reacted to the sound of your father's voice," I told him.

"I know that."

"Maybe he sang something."

Zhepheren looked at me.

"Your father likes to sing, yes? He's always humming after his hunts."

Zhepheren blinked and turned back to the statue. "That would make sense."

"What does he hum? You should hum it now. Perhaps it was an accident, that he activated the Artifact."

Zhepheren gave me a dark look, but I did not care. His father was not the most noble or adventurous of manticores, and that's why the ballad had been written about him, because his journey to the human lands was so unexpected.

"Well?" I asked.

"The story of Cydaniene and Duhonadenu," Zhepheren muttered. He took a few steps away from the statue and began hum the lilting, throaty tune of that old tragedy.

The statue's glow intensified.

"It's working!" I whispered.

Zhepheren's eyes went wide. He hummed more loudly, and then I joined in, as *Cydaniene and Duhonadenu* is meant to be sung by male and female. We swayed together, our voices joining in one great bell-like chime, and the statue glowed so bright that it looked like a star.

And brighter—

And brighter—

And then there was a great, blinding flash of light, and a sudden rush of dry desert heat. I did not know what was happening. I couldn't see anything, or smell anything, or hear anything. There was only a whiteness like the lightning that illuminates the whole sky.

And then I felt a pain in my side.

Fire! My fur was burning, singeing into little black stubs. Smoke twisted around me. I shrieked and tried to run back but I couldn't move. I was too mired in the white light. Distantly I heard Zhepheren crying out.

And then I heard a small whispery human voice—*My lady. My lady, you must run!*

"Ami!" My voice did not seem to work. I tried to trumpet in distress but that did not work either.

The heat burning my fur worked its way up to my wings and my tail. I screamed, because this was not the human lands, this was death.

When I stopped screaming, I was lying among the trees.

My fur was coated with dry dust but not burned at all. Zhepheren sat beside me, whimpering as he licked at his paws. The clearing waited behind us, still flooded with the moonlight. Although the statue didn't glow anymore.

"What happened?" I asked.

Zhepheren didn't answer, but Ami knelt beside me and began stroking my mane. "You were locked in by the magic," she said. "My mother taught me a charm to break those kinds of spells." She gave a weak smile. "I lured you and my lord manticore Zhepheren into the trees, where the magic is not so strong."

"Lured?"

"Yes." She lifted her arm and showed where she had

drawn blood. "The scent brought you to me. I was prepared to run up the trees if I needed to, but you both collapsed when you left the clearing."

I sniffed the air. I could smell the tangy scent of her blood now, but I had not noticed it earlier. There was only the heat and the burning.

"Thank you, servant-human," I said, and I lay my head on my paws. Ami did not stop stroking my mane. "I owe my life to you." I paused. Zhepheren did not seem aware of our conversation, but I lowered my voice to be sure. "Thank you, Ami."

"It is my duty," she said softly, but she smiled a little. Although the magic hadn't worked, and I was still destined to become a ruler of manticores only, I was glad that I was not dead, and that I could do her the honor of calling her by her name.

❧

WE ARRIVED BACK at Father's territory in two days' time, after Zhepheren and I spent the night recovering on the edges of the Oasis. We had not even come to the servants' quarters when we were met by a pair of my father's guards, who were pacing through the outskirts of the wastes.

"Princess Ongraygeeomryn!" shouted the larger of the guards, both of them dropping to their front paws in greeting. Then they straightened and turned to Zhepheren. "You are under arrest by order of the King."

"What!" I cried. "That's not fair!"

"King's orders," the guard said.

Zhepheren did not protest. He did not even arch his tail or bare his teeth. He only settled down in the sand, defeated. He had been quiet on the journey home, padding through the wastes with his head hung low, barely eating the food or drinking the water that Ami divided up for us. Now he seemed to give up completely.

"It was my idea," I said. "I only wished to see the Oasis his father found."

"King's orders," the guard said again. He turned to his partner and they conferred while Zhepheren and Ami and I looked on. My hearing had returned to normal, and I knew they were discussing who would take Zhepheren to the hanging cages and who would accompany me to the palace.

"It's not fair!" I said again, stamping my paws against the ground. "You must imprison me as well!"

"The King wouldn't like that." The smaller guard stepped forward. "I'll be taking you to the palace, my princess."

"No!"

"Ongraygeeomryn," Zhepheren said. I looked at him. He seemed so deflated after our journey. "I failed you. I deserve imprisonment. Please, go."

I started to protest, but the larger guard had arched his tail in Zhepheren's direction, and Zhepheren stood up and began to trudge away from me.

"It really isn't fair," I told my guard.

"It's not my decision, my princess." He nodded and flapped his wings and drew back his tail a little, the poison glistening at the end of the spine. I knew I could not try to free Zhepheren myself; he was a prisoner, and queen's daughter or not, I would be shot by a poisoned spine for helping him escape.

I would have to plead with Father later.

The guard accompanied Ami and me to the rock-nest,

past the servants' quarters and the copse of palm trees where non-royal manticores lived and into the garden. Father and Mother were both there, sitting out in the sun. When I saw them I almost forgot my anger over Zhepheren's arrest, because I was grateful I had not died in the Oasis.

Mother stood up first and let out a great trumpet of joy before bounding across the garden to greet me. We nuzzled each other in the sweet air of the garden.

"What happened?" she cried. "We were so *worried.*"

"I went on an adventure." I flapped my wings, excited to tell her about it—well, about the good parts, not about the failed magic and the fact that I had almost died and consequently had to be saved by a human. I didn't think she would appreciate that.

"An adventure?" Mother pulled away from me, blinking. "What use do you have for an *adventure?* I thought you'd been kidnapped."

Father ambled over beside us, his great muscular bulk casting a dark shadow over our conversation.

"Yes," he said. "We noticed Ashnystion's son went missing the same time you did. Ashnystion is currently in the hanging cages—he refused to confess what he knew."

"What!" My earlier anger exploded out of me. Such injustice! I would never allow such a thing to happen when I was queen. "He didn't confess because he didn't know of our journey. I asked Zhepheren to accompany me to the wastes so we could find the Oasis, like in the ballad."

The garden fell silent. I could smell Ami's fear creeping through the air, although I didn't know what she was frightened of. They wouldn't hurt *her.*

"That's very distressing," Father finally said. "It appears you kidnapped yourself."

I scowled at him. "That doesn't make any sense, Father."

"You're forbidden from leaving our territory. And yet you did, and you bewitched two males into helping you."

Mother made a cautionary whistle in Father's direction, but he ignored her. I pressed myself against the ground, flattening my ears along my skull. Although I was still angry about Zhepheren's imprisonment, I had a feeling this conversation was not going to end well for me, either.

"I'm locking you in the servants' quarters until we decide on further punishment," Father announced.

I hissed in shock.

"Guard, take her and the servant-human." Father flicked his tail dismissively and turned his fierce yellow eyes on me. "You should spend that time considering the effects your actions will have on Ashnystion and Zhepheren."

"That's not fair!" I howled, but the guard had his tail pointed at me again. Ami looked at me with a strange human expression, one I did not understand, and then we walked, defeated, in the direction of the servants' quarters.

❧

I SPENT three days in a room designed for humans, sleeping in the corner or letting me Ami brush my mane with her fingers. It was humiliating. The walls hemmed me in, and I had only a small square window through which to view and smell the outside world. I could not run or hunt, only pace back and forth as Ami sat on the stupid human bed and watched me.

"Do you think they'll kill Zhepheren?" I asked. "Or his father?"

"No, my lady," Ami said. One of the other servant-humans had brought her a bowl of human gruel, and she sat with it balanced on her knee, eating. Mother saw to it that I was given meat, but she had forgotten about Ami. Fortunately, the other servants had not. "I think the King is only upset that you went missing, and when he calms down, my lord manticores Zhepheren and Ashnystion will be released. But you must allow the King time to calm down." She ate another bite of gruel and I wondered if she had known this would happen before we left, if that was why she had been so opposed to the idea.

Ami finished her meal and set the bowl beside the door, where one of the other servant-humans would come to collect it. I collapsed in my usual spot beneath the window, trying to capture the tiny patch of sunlight it let in. Worthless! I wanted to be free, beneath the open sky, not trapped in a clay box like a human.

Ami knelt beside me and began to stroke my mane. I lay my head down on my paws.

"I hope they don't kill them," I said.

"Me too, my lady."

We stayed that way for some time, because there was nothing else to do. The sun moved higher in the sky and my patch of light shifted onto the side of the bed, where I couldn't reach it. I thought about going to sleep.

And then the lock jangled in the door.

I assumed it was the servant-human come to take away Ami's bowl, but instead it was Mother's personal servant-human, opening the door because Mother could not work human technology. I perked up my head—it was too early in the day for meat.

"Ongraygeeomryn," she said, smiling down at me. She

did not step into the room. "Your father has finally changed his mind. You're free to go."

"What!" I leapt to my feet, knocking Ami aside by accident. "Really! No more imprisonment?"

"He thinks you've been punished enough."

I threw back my head and let out a great joyful trumpet, so loud it shook the walls of the room. Then I looked at Mother again. "And what of Zhepheren and Ashnystion? Will they be released?"

"In a few days' time," Mother said. "And Zhepheren now owes Father his life."

I trumpeted again. For Zhepheren to owe Father his life was a minor thing; it meant only that Zhepheren was required to protect Father in battle. But there had not been a battle on our island for ten generations.

"This is the happiest day, Mother!" I reared up on my hind legs and released my wings and trumpeted once more. "Come, servant-human, let's run on the beach to celebrate!"

Ami had gotten to her feet, and she smiled shyly at me through the tangled mat of her hair. "Yes, my lady," she said.

"Don't run into the wastes," Mother commanded, and then she stalked away from the door. I bounded out of the room and through the dark human-smelling hallway and burst out into the sunlight. It was magnificent! Dazzling and bright and everywhere. So unlike the room's shifting patch of sun.

Ami trotted beside me as we made our way down to the beach. The plains of water sparkled in the distance and threw off a salty mist that coated my fur. The air was fresh and clean and even Ami seemed happier, despite the fact that humans do not mind being inside. We wove through the rippling sand dunes, and when we came to the waterline I trumpeted again, my voice ringing out into the sky. I imagined it crossing the plains of water and arriving at the human lands, as if my voice could take my place on that abandoned adventure.

"Shall we race?" I asked Ami.

She nodded without complaint, and I counted off and then took off, kicking up great arcs of sand. I moved ahead of her quickly; racing against a human is not a true race, of course. Manticores are so much stronger and faster. But I slowed down so as not to pull too far ahead, and Ami was quicker than I expected.

I was enjoying the salt and the sun and the clean bright air so much that it took me a moment to realize I had pulled too far ahead of Ami again. I slowed but she didn't catch up. Finally I looked over my shoulder to ensure she hadn't fallen. I found her stopped completely on the sand, gazing at something beyond me.

"Servant-human!" I shouted, my voice rising and falling with the wind. "I command you to race me!"

"Do you see that?" she called back, and pointed.

I turned back around.

I stopped running.

A monster rose up ahead, sharp-clawed and jagged-edged. I let out a soft whimper and cowered back. Ami ran to my side, and we stared at the monster together. Its skin flapped on the wind, the water sloshing around its massive body.

"What is it?" I whispered, my muscles tense and my tail prepared to shoot.

Ami didn't answer right away. She lifted one hand to shield her weak human eyes from the sun. At any moment, I expected the monster to rise to its feet and lumber toward us, roaring and hissing. I arched my spine, straightened my tail.

"It's a ship," Ami said.

"What's that? Will it eat us?"

Ami looked at me. "No, my lady. It's a human vessel. My family has a book with pictures of one."

Books! Some silly human treasure. They brought them to our island many generations ago. I wasn't certain I trusted her assessment.

"There are probably humans on board." Ami's voice sounded strange. Very flat overall, but with a hopefulness shimmering beneath it. I didn't understand. "We should leave now, so they won't hurt you."

"Hurt me! I was to become Queen of the Humans, don't you remember?" I straightened up and crept closer to the monster—the ship. Still it didn't move save for the flaps of skin rippling on the wind. It smelled odd, briny like the beach, but there was a definite undercurrent of human too. Boy-human.

My mouth began to water.

Ami walked with me, her eyes big and round and looking straight ahead. I took this as I sign that the monster was not dangerous, for she had been far more wary at the Oasis, where my life truly had been in danger.

As we approached, the scent of human grew stronger. I licked at my teeth. The meat Mother had brought me the last three days had been most unsatisfactory, as it was dead when she brought it. I hoped Ami was right, that there were humans aboard the ship so I could hunt them and absorb their life's energy into my own body.

And then a small dark figure appeared on the sand, running toward us.

I immediately stopped and crouched down in the sand, my tail lifted.

"Servant-human!" I cried. "You must hide! I'll protect you!"

Ami gave me an inscrutably human look. "I don't believe that will be necessary, my lady."

I snarled a little and pawed at the ground. The figure had slowed his approach, and he lifted his hands when he saw my defensive position. He was now close enough that I could smell the tang of his fear.

"I don't wish to hurt you!" he called out. "Please, girl, call down your pet!"

I realized with a start that he was speaking to Ami! He had recognized us as servant and master, but did not assign the roles correctly.

Ami realized it, too, but her eyes had gone wide again, and she didn't respond. I leapt to my feet, angered by his mistake. "I am not her pet!" I snarled. "She is *my* pet!"

The human leapt backward, kicking up sand. "It can talk!" he shrieked.

"Of course I can talk. Servant-human, stay here." I trotted up to the human, who attempted to scramble backward over the sand. I put my paw on his chest to pin him in place. He gaped at me, his mouth opening and closing the way the humans' always do when we are about to eat them.

"Forgive me," he choked out. "I misread the situation. Please—I can see now that the girl is a servant. I wasn't thinking straight." He bared his teeth at me. No—he was smiling at me. It just didn't look the way it did whenever Ami smiled. "If you let me go, I can offer you great gifts."

My ears perked up when he said *gifts*, but I didn't move my foot away from him. He was an older human, I saw now, which meant his meat would be stringy. However, he had the smell of magic about him, which was what had tantalized me earlier. Wizard-humans are always the most delicious.

"What sort of gifts?" I asked.

"Anything you like," he said. "I'm a peddler of magic. I was sailing from Lisirra to Arkuz when my ship was blown off course during a typhoon. Please, lady, you look as if you'd be a discerning customer."

I recognized the name *Lisirra*. It was part of the human lands, the seat of the human empire. I thought about the blazing light at the Oasis. Perhaps the magic had worked after all, and I really would become queen of the humans.

Keeping the wizard-human pinned, I turned to tell Ami my new revelation, but she had vanished off the beach.

"Looking for your serving-girl?" The wizard-human lifted his head off the sand. I turned to him and snarled, and he dropped back down. "She ran off while we were speaking."

That did not sound like Ami. She was good at obeying. But I couldn't deny that she was no longer on the beach.

"Would you like to hear about my wares?" The wizard-human bared his teeth at me again. "I've got magic from all corners of the globe. Sand-magic from the Empire, swamp-magic from Qilar—I've even managed to capture a bit of the magic of the Jokja Jungle. Most treacherous indeed."

I didn't really understand what he was saying. I didn't recognize any of those names. "Can you take me to the human lands?"

The wizard-human frowned. "Is that what you really wish, my lady manticore?"

Before I could answer, Father's trumpet bellowed up

and down the beach. The wizard-human whimpered beneath me and wriggled against the weight of my paw. I looked over my shoulder. Father and Mother were bounding down the sand, tails and wings raised.

"Ongraygeeomryn!" shouted Mother. "So soon after you were given your freedom?"

"It's just a human," I said.

"Get away from him!" Father ran up beside me, his face twisted into a snarl. The wizard-human went pale. "He could be dangerous."

"Oh, I assure you, lord manticore, I'm no danger, no danger at all. As I was telling this lovely creature, I'm a peddler of magic whose ship was wrecked upon your shores. I'll gladly—"

"You will serve as our meal tonight," Father announced. "Ongraygeeomryn, I demand that you leave this creature at once."

I did not want to go against Father's wishes so soon after the trip into the wastes, so I stepped away, trotting softly over the sand. Ami had appeared at Mother's side, her hair tangled.

"You!" I cried. "Why did you leave?"

"She told us you were in danger," Mother said. "You should be thanking her."

"Danger?" I said. "It's just a wizard-human."

"I didn't like the feel of his magic," Ami said, uneasily. She glanced over at the wizard. "I didn't notice it until he approached, but—Can't you feel it, my lady? It seems—"

"I don't feel anything." I turned away from her. Father had not incapacitated the wizard-human yet. In fact, he didn't even have him pinned. They were talking, as manticore talks to manticore.

"What's happening?" I asked. "Father said the wizard-human was to be our evening meal." I was, in truth, somewhat disappointed in that matter; the wizard-human might have been able to take me to the human-lands, after all.

The wizard-human stood up. Father let him.

Mother bristled beside me. Ami frowned. Together, Father and the wizard-human walked toward us.

"What's this?" Mother asked. "He put our daughter in danger and you haven't even sent him to the hunting fields yet?"

"I won't be sending him to the hunting fields." Father looked at me and Mother in turn, then over to the wizard-human. "Wizard-human Eirnin, tell them what you told me."

The wizard-human Eirnin drew up his chest. "In my travels I have found a way to craft humans out of magic." He stirred his hand over the sand and drew up a glittering figure that spun before us. Mother gasped.

With a flick of his wrist, Eirnin collapsed the figure back into sand.

"Just a taste," he said. "That's not a complete form, of course. With the right magic, I can turn sand into meat." He winked at me. "I can produce humans for you faster than the, ahem, *old-fashioned* way."

I scowled in distaste.

"I've asked him to produce a meal for us tonight," Father said. "If he can do as he claims, we shall make our arrangements."

I could see that Mother did not approve. She clenched her jaw and pawed at the ground. But Father seemed so pleased with himself that she did not protest.

Eirnin looked at all of us in turn: Father, Mother, me, Ami. When his gaze settled on Ami, his smile vanished.

I looked at her. She was glaring at him. I whispered in her ear, "You said he didn't wish to do us harm."

"That was before I sensed *this*," she whispered.

Mother and Father did not pay her any attention, but I could tell that Eirnin had heard her. He took a step toward us. A chill rippled down my spine. His face had changed. He seemed older, and colder, like he was carved out of ice.

"And what, pray tell, did you sense?" he asked.

I stepped in front of her and bared my teeth.

"Ongraygeeomryn!" Father shouted. "I told you, we are going to—"

And then I couldn't hear him anymore. I couldn't hear the beach or the wind. There was only silence.

And then Eirnin lifted his hands and smoke poured out of them.

I knew smoke because the servant-humans used it to cook their meals. This smoke was different, however. It was thick and black and it poured around me and left an oily residue on my fur. As soon it touched me I tried to leap away but I couldn't move. The smoke was so thick it buried Mother and Father and Ami, although not Eirnin, who stared at me as the smoke continued to belch out of his palms.

I thought I heard someone screaming, but then I heard silence. And the smoke poured around and around me. I tried to cry out but it didn't work.

Just like the Oasis, I thought.

And then there was nothing.

"Manticore! Open your eyes."

I was dreaming of the garden outside the rock-nest, dreaming of Zhepheren and Ami chasing and playing with me amongst the flowers. It was quite a lovely dream. But then a harsh human voice interrupted it.

"I command you, open your eyes!"

My eyes opened. I was not in the garden. I was in a cage. All around me was the sky and the scent of the beach. And long wooden planks, laid out flat like the stone floors of the servants' quarters.

I tried to stand up, but my legs collapsed beneath me.

"Yes, yes, I'm afraid you won't be doing much of that the next few days." Eirnin's face loomed in front of my cage. I snarled at him, but it came out a whimper, sad and pathetic, and when I tried to shoot a spine at him nothing happened.

"What have you done?" I asked.

He didn't answer, only opened a latch at the top of my cage and dropped in a bloody animal's leg. It landed next to my head with a wet *thump*.

"What am I supposed to do with this?"

"Eat it." When Eirnin closed the lock of my cage, energy rippled over me. Magic. I wished Ami was here, to tell me if it was dangerous or not.

"I hunt my meals."

Eirnin shrugged. "Not anymore, you don't."

He walked away.

I sniffed at the leg. It did smell fresh, although not the

fresh of a kill I had completed myself. I licked at it, tasting the steely blood. It didn't taste right—too wild, too salty. And I wasn't terribly hungry anyway.

I nudged it away and curled up into a ball. The cage rocked back and forth, a movement I found uncomfortable. I found that laying my head down helped.

Much time passed. The sun rose high in the sky and then lowered itself. The shadows shifted. Eventually, I grew hungry enough to gnaw at the animal leg, although the constant motion made my stomach roll around. I could not see much from my vantage point in the cage, and I could see less still when I had to stay lying down, but I did notice tall trees growing out of the wooden floor, their leaves wide and pale. I could feel the magic. It was heavy and oily like the smoke that had consumed me before, and it coated everything.

When the sky began to glow orange, Eirnin came to my cage again. This time, he had a bowl of water, which he lowered in using the human invention of a rope and lever. I could not attack him.

"Sorry," he said. "Meant to bring that to you earlier."

I stared down at the water, at my own wavering reflection.

"Why are you doing this?" I asked him. "My father did you a great honor! He offered you a place among his court, serving us, and you repay him by stealing me?"

Eirnin crossed his arms over his chest. The wind ruffled his gray hair.

"I shall refuse to drink!" I said. "I shall waste away here in my cage."

"You'll do no such thing," he said, and for a moment the feeling of magic intensified, and I knew it to be true: I would eat, and drink. He compelled it. But I would attack him, with tooth and claw, if ever I had the chance. His magic might have disarmed my tail, but he did not disarm the rest of me. "As for you question—your father was a fool."

I growled at him, deep in my throat.

"He believed my story! About the bumpkin peddler." Eirnin laughed. "You did too, I suppose. The little human girl was the only one who saw through it. Why she tried to save you—" Eirnin shook his head. "You know she was going to barter her way onto my ship, yes? When she first saw me? Before she recognized my magic."

I thumped my useless tail against the floor. It made a hollow echoing sound.

"Ami would not abandon me," I said.

"Don't be so sure." Eirnin wagged his finger. "No servant wants to stay a servant forever. But alas, she would rather stay with manticores than travel the seas with me. And that, my lady manticore, should tell you everything you need to know."

I didn't understand. Ami was happy serving me, surely. She had saved my life. Twice!

Eirnin left, and I could not ask him any more questions.

Night fell. I slept and woke up aching. In the thin morning light, I was able to stand up without collapsing, and the cage's motion did not bother me so much. I could still smell the beach, and it occurred to me, now that my head had cleared some, that we must be traveling across the water plains.

A ship, Ami had called Eirnin's monster. I did not understand the word. But it was a sort of water-nest, a place to live as we traveled over the waves.

Not long after I woke, Eirnin brought me another

animal leg. This one did not smell as fresh, but it did not smell rotten, either, and so I ate it, as his magic compelled me to do. I drank his water as well. He sat several paces away from me and watched.

"Well?" I said when I had finished. "Will you answer my question now?"

"What question?" he asked, all innocence.

"The one I've repeatedly asked you! What have you done? Why have you done it?"

"I told you yesterday."

"You told me nothing. You said my father was a fool, and you said you were a filthy lying human."

"I don't think I said *quite* that much." Eirnin smiled. "But I suppose that's fair, I didn't quite explain. And what is there to explain? Quite honestly, I'm fulfilling your wish."

"I never wished this!"

"You wished to travel to the human lands," he said.

With that sentence, my heart almost stopped. "The human lands," I whispered.

He nodded. "That's where I'm taking you." He shrugged. "In a way, at least."

"But why!" I shrieked, launching myself at the bars of the cage. They rattled and thrummed with magic. And held.

"Because I need a manticore," Eirnin said. "Manticore blood has a particular sort of magic in it. You can't find it anywhere else. Has to be living blood, unfortunately, which is why I'm keeping you alive." He smiled again. "I won't extract much at a time, my lady manticore. You've nothing to fear. I know the ship is uncomfortable, but I've a nice nest prepared for you on my island."

I roared, a great trumpeting cry that echoed out into the sky. But Eirnin didn't even blink.

"I'm afraid there isn't much you can do," he said, "other than roar."

And then he walked away.

I collapsed at the bottom of my cage. Manticores do not cry; that is a human oddity. But I could see why humans did it, if crying would relieve this horrible weight inside my chest. I buried my face in my paws and trembled. The human lands. Eirnin was taking me to the human lands.

A thought materialized in the back of my head, a cold and terrible thought: that I had brought this fate upon myself, when I visited the Oasis, when I wished upon the Artifact to be taken across the water plains. But it was not supposed to be this way. It had not happened this way for Zhepheren's father. He had not been *lost*.

I let these thoughts consume me only for a brief time. Eventually, I pushed my sorrow away. Manticores are not built for sorrow. Eirnin was nowhere to be seen, although I could smell him, faintly, through the wood. I stood up. Arched my spine and flapped my wings. Drew my claws across the bars of the cage. The magic rippled.

Eirnin was the source of the magic.

If Eirnin died, the magic died with him.

We made our way across the plains of water, the sky a deep and unending blue overhead. And I paced in my cage, and I waited, and I planned.

Someday, I would escape.

The End

The Automaton's Treasure

I sat on the deck of the *Ocean's Rose* with the only book I'd managed to shove in my trunk before I had to leave my homeland forever: an illustrated history of the Qilari swamps. It was an old book, a gift from some visiting dignitary or another who had heard about my love of the swamps. When I was a little girl, I'd been mad about them. I thought I'd outgrown the obsession, but banishment will send you wheeling back to your childhood, apparently.

I was sitting in one of the rickety wooden chairs left out for passengers, alone except for the handful of sailors scrambling in the ropes overhead. The book lay open in my lap, but I couldn't concentrate on the words. I'd read it twice on this trip already, and there were still another two months before we landed in Lisirra, the city that would serve as my prison.

A family came up on deck, shattering the peaceful, windy silence. They looked Empire, like most of the people on this ship, and they had a tottering little boy who ran up to the railing and peered over the edge, shouting about sharks. His mother joined him, saying something I couldn't make out over the wind. They were speaking the Empire tongue, which was my entire reason for eavesdropping. I'd certainly need to be fluent soon enough.

The wind picked up and turned the pages of my book, landing on a dog-eared illustration of the Qilari crocodile, mean-faced and spiky-tailed. I shut the book and settled back in my chair. The masts were silhouetted in the sun. Two sailors scurried along the tops of the sails, shouting to each other. Empire again, although a dialect I wasn't familiar with. I caught every three or four words—*ship, sight, direction. Cannons.*

Cannons? My Empire was rustier than I thought. The *Ocean's Rose* was a passenger ship, and decidedly not one for aristocrats or the wealthy. I doubted they had cannons on board.

The two sailors were joined by a third, a woman who swung in on a rope. She landed lightly on her feet, balancing herself against the top of the mast. I couldn't see her face, but she nodded her head vigorously and then swooped away again, dropping to the deck a few paces away from me and rushing off toward the captain's quarters.

The family was still standing by the railing. They'd been looking down at the sea, not up at the sky, and missed that bit of excitement.

And then an officer came on deck.

He walked over to the family first and spoke to them in a slow, hushed tone. I tilted my head toward them, trying to be inconspicuous, but I couldn't hear. The mother and father exchanged brief, worried glances; the son was still clinging to the railing. A pause. Then the mother wrapped her arm around her son's shoulders and led him away, speaking to him as she did so. I caught, "a bit of time down below—" before the officer appeared next to my chair, the chain draped around his shoulder glittering in the sun.

"Good afternoon, Lady Anaja-tu," he said.

"That's not my name," I snapped, more harshly than I'd intended.

He faltered. I'd confused him. "Excuse me," he said. "My, ah, lady—"

I scowled, but I didn't correct him a second time.

"I'm afraid we'll be sailing into a storm soon. We're asking that all passengers retire belowdeck. I'll send a porter around when it's safe for you to come back up."

"A storm?" The sky was a blank curve of blue, like the side of a flawless Saelini glass vase. "Are there even any *clouds* out?"

"Yes," he said, his voice firm. "We have a soothsayer on board, my lady, and these storms can form without warning, this far out."

I'd studied enough science at university to know that storms don't materialize out of an empty sky, but I didn't say anything. Perhaps magic was involved. If that was the case, then I didn't think going belowdeck would do much good, but—

I remembered the sailors shouting the word *cannon*.

"It's not a storm, is it?"

The officer gazed at me with a polite and quietly desperate expression. "I really must insist you go down below, my lady."

I hadn't felt anything since I'd left the port at Arkuz, watching Father disappear into a point as we sailed away, and I didn't feel anything now. I stood up and tucked my book under my arm. The wind smelled of the ocean, not of rain, but I was aware of a flurry of activity in the masts overhead. Shouts of profanity and fear and protection charms.

"Fine," I said.

I went down below. Father had arranged for a private cabin, the last gift he ever gave me. It was large enough that if I lay flat on my back my feet would touch one end and the top of my head the other, but right now it felt claustrophobic and dark despite the magic-cast lantern swinging in the corner. I pulled out my trunk and rifled through its belongings, looking for something that might work as a weapon. The closest I found was a decorative hairpin, a long silver spike topped with jeweled flowers. *She* had given it to me, a sign that she knew who I really was, a sign that she was officially in on the joke. Some joke, that got me kicked out of my homeland.

I shoved my trunk back into place, pulled down my cot, and stretched out on my back, holding the hairpin to my chest.

And waited.

The ship rocked along, as calm as always. Occasionally feet pounded overhead, and the lantern would flare and then sputter—magic working its way through the walls.

I wrapped my fingers more tightly around the hairpin, the jewels digging into my palm. I closed my eyes, whispered her name.

Silence.

Silence.

Silence.

And then:

A loud, cracking *boom*.

I sat up as the boat jerked and tilted. My head slammed

against the wall. Spots of light flared everywhere. The hairpin clattered to the ground, and I cried out and launched myself at the floor, feeling around for it in the murky shadows. The lantern was almost completely depleted.

Another round of cannon fire. The ship didn't move this time. My fingers closed in on the pin, and I brought it up just as the lantern failed.

Footsteps: pounding, frantic. Men screaming. Pistol shots. I sat hyperventilating in the dark, holding onto the hairpin as if it were her hand.

Cannon fire reverberated up from the floorboards. But the boat didn't jerk and shudder. We weren't hit.

The door to my cabin flew open.

I screamed, cowered back on my cot. A man stood in the doorway, a magic-cast lantern in one hand and a sword in the other.

"Oh shut up." He stepped inside and kicked the door closed. With his sword, he knocked down the original lantern and hung his in its place. The light was different, greenish-blue instead of white.

I shoved myself up into the corner. "Take what you want!" I shouted, kicking at my trunk. "You can have it all!" That wasn't entirely true; I'd claw his eyes out before I let him have the hairpin.

He laughed. "That ain't why we're here." The light in the lantern brightened momentarily, and I got my first good look at him: He was tall, bony, and Jokjani, although he wore a ragged Empire jacket. He paced around the cabin as he talked, his sword out, his hand on the butt of his pistol. "Just looking to take the boat. Old one don't meet with the captain's needs."

The cannon fire had stopped.

"Are you going to kill me?"

"What?" The pirate stopped. "Kill you? No, not unless you do something stupid. Captain don't like killing non-Confederates. That's you, sweetheart."

I'd read enough pirate stories to know what the Confederation was. I glared at him, which just made him laugh again.

"We'll drop you off first port we come to. Starlight Rock, most like."

"Is that in the Empire?"

The pirate looked at me for a moment and then burst into laughter. "No, girl, it ain't in the Empire. Pirates' island, and not much there but starlight and rocks. Hence the name." He gave a little flourish as he said that last part, but my body felt like it'd been emptied out. Some abandoned pirates' island was even worse than landing in Lisirra. It was a true prison.

"You'll stay locked up in your cabins till then. Sailors got a choice of joining up or not, course. Now, if one of 'em says no—" The pirate drew a line across his throat. "Well, we drown 'em, usually, but—"

"Why are you in my room?" I didn't want to hear any more about murdering sailors.

The pirate grinned. "To keep you secure till things get settled. Ain't gonna touch you, if that's what you're worried about."

I shuddered and drew my knees up to my chest. I didn't let go of the hairpin. The pirate tapped his sword against the side of my trunk. He looked bored.

"How long's that going to take?" I said.

"Don't go planning anything." He looked at me. "I told you, we're gonna let you go."

"On a *pirates' island.*"

"Better than the middle of the ocean."

He was right, of course. I couldn't imagine them just letting us go, but it also seemed like if this pirate was to kill me, he would have done it already.

"Couple hours," he said.

"What?"

"How long it's gonna take." He shrugged. "Till we got the new crew sorted. And then we'll be on our way."

He looked up at me and grinned, his face splitting into two, and the green light carved his face into shadows.

❧

I spent the next days locked in my cabin, just as the pirate promised. Someone brought food twice a day, once in the morning and once in the evening. Decent stuff, thin stews and hard little scones. I supposed they were feeding us from the ship's stores.

Different pirates would drop off the food, and I recognized most as sailors from when the ship had been a passenger liner. One of them even handed me a tin cup full of sugar-wine one evening. "Drink up, sister," he said, lounging in the doorway, lips curled in a mocking smile. "Got another month before we get to Starlight Rock."

Another month, and cabin fever was already crawling over my skin. They let us out once a day, in groups of three or four, to go up on deck and empty our chamber pots into the ocean. A pirate would keep his pistol trained on us the whole time, and we never got to stay out for long. But it was long enough for me to remember what the sun felt like.

Because I couldn't keep track of sunrise and sunset, I marked off meals and times spent up above in the flyleaf of my illustrated history of the swamp. Eight meals. Four times allowed on deck. Four days.

In those long stretches of time between meals and deck time, I lay on my cot and watched patterns of light and shadow form across the ceiling. I thought of *her*, the person I loved, the person I'd left behind, the person who'd cost me my homeland. I took all of my belongings out of my trunk and arranged them on the floor and stared at them like they were tea leaves and could tell me what the future held.

Nothing. The future held nothing.

During this fruitless exercise, I found a thin sheet of paper tucked into the bottom of the trunk. I hadn't put it there. When I unfolded it I found a list of names written in Father's neat hand. *These men can help you*, he'd written across the bottom. *Contact them when you arrive in Lisirra.*

I stared at the list of names for a long time. My eyes felt heavy but I didn't cry. For the last month, I'd been dreading my arrival in the hot, dry city of Lisirra. I couldn't imagine my life beyond the days spent aboard the *Ocean's Rose*. But then the pirates came, and now I could hardly picture my life at all.

Rage flashed through me: at myself, at the pirates, at Father. I crumbled the list of names into a ball and hurled it at the wall. It bounced off and tumbled across the floor. I picked up the illustrated history of Qilar and flung it open to a random page, trying to distract myself. It opened on an image of a cypress tree, roots disappearing beneath the calm, smooth surface of the swamp.

Father put me on a boat to Lisirra when he should have put me on a boat here, to the swamps. Jokja is often called a Free Country because it's not part of the Empire, but the swamps are true free places, belonging to no king or queen or lord. Just like me.

I slammed the book shut and slid it away. Then I curled up on my cot and stared into the gloomy darkness.

I waited to die.

✦

A WEEK PASSED, according to my notes in the illustrated history. I ate twice a day; I visited topside once a day. I thought I might go mad from boredom.

And then one night I had a visitor.

I was sleeping when it happened; whether it was actually night or not, I have no way of knowing. I woke suddenly in the green darkness, gasping for breath. I'd heard something. A clatter.

I lay in the darkness, breathing hard, listening.

It happened again. A *click click click* like tumbling stones. I sucked in all my breath and held it, fingers curling around the thin woolen blanket that came with my room.

Click click click.

And then something scuttled across the floor.

"Who the hell's there!" I shouted, sitting up. The scuttling stopped. I wished I had some control over the lantern, but it always cast the same murky light. "Show yourself!"

A long pause. I stared into the darkness and slipped my hand under my pillow, where I kept the hairpin.

"Come on, then!"

A figure emerged out of the shadows. Small and low to

the ground like a weasel. I watched it move in wide ambling steps across the floor. Then it crawled on top of my trunk.

I shrieked and dropped my hairpin.

It looked exactly like a Qilari crocodile, only it was much too small and crafted out of gold and shining jewels. When it moved, its scales parted, revealing flashes of the clockwork underneath.

It stared at me for some time.

"What are you?" I whispered in Jokjani.

A pause. Then it opened it opened its mouth with a steaming hiss.

"Are you *magic?*"

It worked its jaw up and down, but I heard only a rumbling, unintelligible clatter. It stopped, shook out its head, tiny clawed hands pressing against its cheeks. Then it looked at me again, and spoke: "You—not-thief—"

I couldn't understand the rest. It spoke in the southern dialect of Qilari, the language spoken in the swamps, and half its words were garbled by that horrible clacking.

"Forgive—hurt—bad man—" The creature jumped off the trunk and scurried across the floor toward my cot, startling me with its quickness. It stood up on its hind legs and peered at me. Its eyes were star sapphires, and they possessed a brightness that made me think of living things.

"You—not-thief—"

"No, I'm not a thief," I said in my own halting Qilari. The creature seemed to understand me. It crawled onto the cot beside me and leaned in close to my face. I was afraid to look away.

Then it let out a stream of clattering Qilari I could hardly follow.

"Slow down!" I said. "I can't understand you."

"Yes," it said. "Broke me."

"Broke you? Someone broke you?"

"Yes. The thief." The creature dropped away from me, down to all fours. "I am Safin." It seemed to gesture at itself. I was beginning to understand it better.

"Safin? Is that your name?"

"Yes. Your name?"

I hesitated, but the creature—Safin—kept staring at me, and I thought maybe I was dreaming anyway. "Marjani."

Safin nodded, satisfied, and dropped down to the floor.

"Nice to—converse—" he said. His voice garbled again. "Come back again?"

I nodded, dumbly, and Safin slid away into the shadows.

❧

Safin returned two nights later, once again waking me from a fitful sleep. I rolled over on my side and found him sitting underneath the magic-cast lantern, the light oxidizing his golden scales.

"Hello," he said. His voice was clearer now, less garbled.

"Hello." I sat up and drew the blanket around me. Safin watched me with his crocodile's grin.

"I'm not dreaming, am I?" I asked.

Safin tilted his head. "Dream? No, this is not a dream."

We stared at each other.

"What *are* you?" I finally blurted, and then cringed for a moment, expecting a reprimand for my rudeness. But I was a prisoner aboard a pirate ship, talking with a magical arti-fact. Rudeness was the least of my concerns.

"I am an automaton." He waddled up to my cot and

reared up on his hind legs, his eyes appearing over the cot's edge. "I was stolen and brought onboard this ship."

"Oh." An automaton. I'd heard about them, when I studied at university—they were magician's business, a specialty of metal-magic. Artifacts infused with sorcery. "I can understand you better tonight."

"Yes. I was able to do some repairs."

Silence fell over us. The ship rocked back and forth, wood creaking. I could hear the ocean on the other side of my wall, but it seemed lost to me. All I knew was this little room.

"I was taken from my great treasure," Safin said. "By a thief. But the thief is dead now."

I shivered. "The pirates?"

"He tried to escape during the battle, to barter his way onto the other ship. Such terror! Guns firing and the smoke from the cannons. I did not have the words at the time, but I've learned them since. He was shot. He threatened to kill some important man."

Safin reported this all in a clicking, mechanical voice, as calm as if he were reporting the weather. I'll admit I found it reassuring that this thief wasn't killed on a whim. I'd taken for granted, naively, that the pirates really did plan to drop us at Starlight Rock.

"I escaped during the madness, but I am still trapped. I long to return to my great treasure." Safin dropped down on all fours and crawled away from the cot, pacing in circles around my cabin. "My great treasure! You would not be able to help me, would you?"

I pulled the blanket tighter around my shoulders. It wasn't cold in the cabin, only damp and dark, but I was shivering anyway. "I'm as trapped as you are, I'm afraid. Worse, because I can't leave here unless they let me."

But Safin didn't seem to hear me. He stopped pacing and stood facing the door, one foot lifted up, his tail sticking straight out.

"Safin?" I asked hesitantly.

He opened his mouth and hissed, a long, low, steaming sound. My heartbeat raced, my mouth went dry.

The lantern flickered.

"Must hide!" he shrieked. "Keep me secret!"

"What do you—"

He scurried up the wall, squeezing through a narrow gap in the corner of the ceiling and disappearing.

I was alone again.

I sighed and slumped back against the wall. The lantern swung back and forth, growing dimmer and dimmer. Stupid, worthless thing.

And then lines appeared on my floor.

They glowed with magic-light—a bright white-blue, not murky green. They crisscrossed over my floor, forming lopsided loops around the cabin, tracing over the wall, to the gap where Safin had disappeared.

Someone banged on my door.

I jolted and sat up, disoriented by the noise and the veins of white light crossing over my cabin.

A jingle of keys in the lock. The door swung open.

"Dinner already?" I said.

A pirate stepped into my cabin—a woman. I recognized her as the sailor I'd seen swinging through the ropes the day the ship was attacked.

"I'll be damned, he has been in here." The woman stomped into my cabin, pistol drawn.

"Hey!" I shouted. "What are you doing?"

The woman stopped and looked at me for the first time. She was Empire, black hair hanging in a single thick braid down her spine, and she looked nothing like the aristocratic women I was used to.

"You see all this?" She gestured at the lines with her pistol. "This means the little shit has been in your cabin. Where is he?"

"The little shit?"

She sighed. I kept my eye on her pistol, although she didn't seem to have an inclination to point it at me.

"It's a machine," she said. "Runs on magic. Looks like a crocodile."

"I haven't seen anything like that." I'd had plenty of experience with lying, and I knew to look her straight in the eye, to steady my breathing.

"It's been in here."

"I've been asleep," I said. "It might've been in here, but I haven't seen it."

She stood with her weight on one foot and studied me, eyes flicking over my face. I didn't flinch away.

"You aren't going to find anyone who could break it down on Starlight Rock, so no use hiding him," she said. "Have to undo the magic first, and there aren't many there who can work that sophisticated of magic."

"I have no idea what you're talking about." But as I spoke I thought about Safin's golden scales, his inlaid jewels. He'd fetch quite the price if he were in pieces.

He must have felt the tracking spell. No wonder he fled.

The woman gave me another hard look. "You sure about that?"

"I swear it. I've never seen a magical crocodile in my life."

The boat rocked, the lantern swung, the lines of Safin's footsteps glowed.

"We'll see," she said, and then she left my cabin, slamming the door shut behind her.

***

OUR JOURNEY to Starlight Rock progressed as it always had, but now my days were punctuated not only by meals and trips up above, but also by visits from Safin, who crept into my room with news about the ship.

"The captain never leaves his quarters unless the moon is out," he told me. "The crew is bored. The other passengers cry a lot. Hafsa is angry she hasn't caught me yet."

Hafsa was the woman who had slammed into my cabin that night. Safin talked about her almost as much as he talked about his great treasure back in Qilar.

"She wants to sell me in Lisirra," he said. "Just like the thief."

"She can't sell you if you hasn't caught you."

"But she'll catch me eventually, yes? I can disembark with you at Starlight Rock, and together we can return to my great treasure!"

He was so convinced I could save him that it made my heart ache. "I imagine they'll be looking for you when we leave the ship," I said. "Or Hafsa will, anyway."

Safin hung his head. His expression never changed—always the same gleaming eyes, the same toothy grin. But I'd talked with him enough that I could see the other ways he revealed his feelings.

"I can't stay aboard," he said. "You are the only one who can converse in Qilari. Who else will help me?"

I crossed my arms over my chest and looked away from him. A year ago I had dreams of swooping in and saving *her*, taking her away from the palace, running off into the Jokja Jungle together. But now I couldn't even save myself. That Safin thought I could save him was laughable. Ridiculous.

"You can try and disembark," I said. "But unless your great treasure's on Starlight Rock, we won't get to it."

"It's in Qilar!"

I sighed. "I *know* that. I'm just saying— " He was up on his hind legs, pressing his front claws into the side of my cot. "We would need a ship."

"We have a ship here."

"*We* don't have anything."

Safin looked at me for a moment longer, blinking. Then he dropped down to the floor and paced. I could imagine the lines appearing the next time Hafsa cast a tracking spell.

"Do you want to go to Starlight Rock?" he asked, still moving.

"Of course not. I'm not sure there's even food there. Or anything." This past month I had done everything in my power not to think about the future. But we were getting close. I knew that. Safin had told me; he'd overhead the crew talking.

"Then don't go." He stopped and looked at me again.

"I'm a prisoner," I said, irritated. "I have no choice." Just like the rest of my life. No choice in leaving Jokja. No choice in who I loved.

Safin didn't answer. I flopped down on my back and stared at the ceiling and listened to the grind of his gears as he walked in circles. Then there was a great bellowing hiss and suddenly Safin pounced on my stomach.

"Hey!" I scrambled to push him off, but he dug his claws into my dress and held on tight. "Let go!"

"You must stay onboard the ship," he said. "That's the only way. Stay onboard and tell the captain we must go to Qilar. Lie if necessary. The great treasure is waiting, and after I am reunited with it, then you can find your way to Idai City. Yes, yes. What do you say?"

"I say that's impossible," I told him, and shoved him to the floor. This time, he didn't argue.

⊗

THE DAY we arrived at Starlight Rock I woke with dread in my bones. Safin had not come to visit me the night before and I slept soundly, but when I woke to the clamor of bells that morning, I knew: We had found land. And my life was lost.

I didn't know if they would let us take our possessions, but I packed my things anyway, all my worn and filthy clothes, the useless list of names Father had given me, my illustrated history of southern Qilar. The hairpin I wore like armor, sliding it into the coil of braids at the back of my neck.

I sat on my cot and waited. My body was numb; my thoughts were hollow. The bells clanged and clanged.

I didn't have to wait long. A knock came at my door, and the lock jangled.

Hafsa waited on the other side.

She didn't say anything and her gun was put away. But when I saw her, I thought of Safin: *You must stay onboard the ship.*

A complete impossibility without leverage. And I had

49

no leverage. My title was lost; my most expensive possession was a hairpin I refused to part with.

But maybe I didn't need a possession.

"Come on," Hafsa said. "We're here. Bring what you can carry. The porter's long gone."

I didn't move from the cot.

"Did you hear me?" she asked, hand moving toward her pistol.

"Yes." It came out quiet, almost a whisper. "I—the thing you were looking for it. I saw it last night."

She froze. I forced myself to look away from her pistol and into her face.

"You're right, he had been coming to my room. I couldn't sleep last night and I—I actually saw him."

She dropped her hand to her side and looked me up and down. "What do you want?"

"What?"

"You want something out of this. Go on and tell me, and I'll see what I can do."

I took a deep breath and reminded myself that my life was over regardless. "I want passage to Qilar."

She blinked at me and then threw back her head and laughed. "We don't need the gold that bad, girlie."

"No, you don't understand." The words spilled out of me, and I thought of the deception that I had gotten me banished, how easy that had been as well. "The automaton— his name is Safin, he told me that—he's part of a great treasure. And he wants to get back to it, more than anything."

The ship tilted, and Hafsa shot out one hand to steady herself against the doorframe. "Go on."

"If you told him you were returning him to his great treasure, he'd help you find it, I'm sure. And the treasure's in

Qilar, in the swamps, so—" I shrugged. "As payment for helping you find it, you can drop me off at Port Idai." When she arched an eyebrow, I added, "Or whatever's convenient."

We stared at each other in the creaking silence.

"Wait here," she said, and she slammed and locked the door.

I let out a long breath and slumped against the wall. Sweat dripped down my spine.

"Marjani!"

I looked up at the gap in the ceiling. Safin's head appeared.

"Wonderful thinking!" he cried.

"Were you in there the whole time?"

"Oh, yes. I knew you'd devise something!"

"Look," I said, standing up on the coat so I could lower my voice. "She's probably going to ask me to find you. I don't want to do it here—too suspicious. I'll wander the boat a bit and call your name, and you come out before they hurt me. Do you understand?"

"Yes, yes!" He disappeared, and I collapsed down on the cot. I didn't think this was going to work. I was acting by rote, an automaton myself.

Hafsa returned. "The other passengers are disembarking now. You have until the last one is off the ship to find the creature."

My head spun. "How long will that be?"

"I don't know. But you better look fast. And don't try anything, either." She pulled out her pistol and made a show of packing in the powder and the shot. "I'll be right there with you."

"What if it won't come out because you're with me?"

"Then off to the Rock with you." She grinned, balancing

her pistol over one shoulder. I couldn't believe she'd been a run-of-the-mill sailor a month ago.

"Fine." I stood up, straightening my spine, lifting my chin. Funny how all those years of etiquette lessons became useful.

Hafsa held the door for me, and I stepped out into the corridor. It was as dank as always, but I could hear voices overhead, chattering and fearful.

"Safin!" I called out, winding down the hallway, Hafsa right behind me. "Safin! I've found a way to get you home!"

I didn't know where I was going. I followed the twist of the corridor. We passed clumps of pirates, and they stared at me, leering. "Safin!"

"Here, my lady!" We were in the mostly empty storeroom, and he dropped out of the ceiling and landed on my shoulder. I bit back a scream. "Ready to serve you, Lady Marjani."

"You can understand that?" Hafsa asked.

"It's southern Qilari." I turned to her. Safin draped over my shoulders like a stole. "He said he's ready to serve me."

Hafsa stared at me—at Safin—with a mercenary glint in her eye. "I can't believe it," she said. "How *easy*—" She shook her head. "Well, they're still disembarking, so you may have found a ticket to Qilar after all. Ask it if it knows the way to the treasure."

I did. Safin said, "Of course I know the way! We talked—"

"He knows," I said to Hafsa.

"Yeah, we'll, it better be able to prove it. Come on."

We went up above. The sun was high in the sky and bright, and it bounced off Safin's scales and into my eyes. A few of the passengers waiting along the railing turned and looked at me, frowning. We were at a dock, I saw, that led into a shabby little town. Lush green trees rose up behind it.

"The name isn't really accurate," Hafsa said. "But you'd be better off in Qilar."

She poked me in the back with her pistol, shoving me toward the captain's quarters. She didn't knock, just walked in and gestured for me to follow. The windows were pinned with thick, dark fabric, blocking out the sun. Magic-cast lanterns glowed in the corners, casting a cleaner version of the green light I'd grown so accustomed to.

No one waited for us in the front room.

"Sit down," she said, pointing with her gun to a row of chairs. "And don't let the thing escape."

I slid into one of the chairs, and Safin dropped down into my lap as Hafsa left, closing the door behind her.

"Is it working?" he asked. "I cannot speak Empire."

"So far," I said. "They're going to make you show them the way."

"To the great treasure? Oh, delight! I will be reunited."

Footsteps. I looked up, one hand resting on Safin's back. Hafsa came into the room and stepped to the side. A man followed her. He was tall and stooped, straggly gray hair falling into his face. When he looked at me I gasped, because his eyes were a pale cold gray I'd never seen before, and I felt them trap me like chains.

"So it looks like you've captured our little friend." He walked up to me, his movements measured and graceful. Safin trembled against my lap, his gears clicking. "We were going to chop him up, but I hear tell of a great treasure?"

I nodded and tried to keep my voice strong. "Yes. Sir. In southern Qilar."

The captain dragged a chair and sat down so that he was facing me. "Is this a trick, girl?"

I shook my head, aware that he was staring at me. Studying me. My thoughts felt suddenly cold, and I went still and focused only on those times Safin told me of his treasure.

He nodded, satisfied. The cold in my head dissipated.

"I guess we can make sail for Qilar. Might be a good idea anyway, what with Captain Lao still on our asses." He glanced at Hafsa. "Ain't that right?"

"It is, sir."

He turned to me. I tried not to look at his eyes but they seemed to loom in his face, threatening to overwhelm me. "You are now a crew of the pirate ship *Ocean's Dagger*. You that nobleman's daughter I heard some of the sailors talking about? Lady Anaja-tu?"

I hated hearing that name aloud. "That isn't my name anymore, sir."

He laughed. "That's the spirit. So what is your name, then?"

"Marjani."

"Just Marjani. Good enough for me. You ever take a yacht up the royal river, Marjani?"

"Once or twice." I kept stroking Safin's back like he was a cat, and his tail curled around my wrist. It was the only thing keeping me calm.

"Eh, maybe we can teach you a bit about the ropes. Till then, you'd best learn how to handle a mop and broom. Hafsa here can show you."

I expected Hafsa to protest, but she didn't.

"We'll leave here in a week's time," he said, standing up. "You aren't confined to your cabin any longer but you also can't leave the ship, do you understand? You try, I'll shoot you myself."

"Yes, sir," I whispered.

If my fear amused him, he didn't show it. "Same thing holds true if we get to Qilar and there's no treasure." He pointed at my forehead with his finger. "The bullet will go right there."

I nodded, tightened my grip on Safin, who snuggled against me.

"Very well." He shoved his chair back into place and ambled over to the door leading into the back part of his quarters. "Always was a bit of risk taker." He nodded at Hafsa and disappeared through the doorway.

Seven days later, we were on our way.

THREE MONTHS PASSED.

My time onboard the *Ocean's Dagger* was markedly different from my time aboard the *Ocean's Rose*. Although I wasn't condemned to my cabin, I was condemned in other ways—to polishing the wood on the deck until it shone in the sun, or to helping the cook prepare food for the crew. Hafsa, the closest I had to a human friend, spent most of her time up in the masts, but she was kind enough to me in the evenings, when the crew would while the hours away with music and drinking and dancing. Those nights were the only times I ever saw the captain. Safin had been right: he only left his quarters under the cover of moonlight, and he would stand off to the side and watch the carousing with his arms crossed over his chest, never joining in.

He frightened me. But he seemed to frighten everyone

except Rafi, the first mate who commanded the ship in his stead.

The day we spotted land was windy and humid and overcast, and the entire crew was in a lazy, indolent mood. I was supposed to be mopping the upper deck, but instead I was looking down at the green-gray ocean, Safin at my side. I hadn't seen much of him during those three months, but the last few days he'd come creeping out of his hiding places, asking if we had arrived yet. Now he was pacing around my feet, chattering to himself about his great treasure.

The warning bells rang thrice in quick succession. I jumped and grabbed my mop as if it were a weapon, the muscles in my back tense and ready for a fight. Safin stopped his pacing and stood up on his hind legs, head swinging back and forth.

"What do the bells mean?" he asked.

"I'm not sure." But then I noticed that the crew were scrambling up in the masts, looking to the east, and they seemed in high spirits. Land, I remembered. The bells meant land.

I ran around to the port side, and Safin followed, his claws clicking against the deck.

Off on the horizon, peeking through the wispy gray clouds, was a narrow line of green.

"Land? Oh, great treasure!" The automaton leapt up on the railing in his excitement, and I clapped my hands down on his sides to keep him from falling into the water. The land was far off enough to seem like a dream, but I could not stop staring at it. I'd forgotten what it was to stand on an unmoving surface.

"That's not Qilar proper." It was Hafsa. She leaned up against the railing beside me, the wind blowing her hair away from her face. "You have to pass a handful of these narrow little islands before you get to the river mouth. And that's how we get to the great treasure, isn't it, little automaton?"

I translated her question, and Safin nodded. "The river will take you to the great treasure, oh yes."

"It is," I told her. "How much longer until we get there? To the river's mouth?"

She shrugged. "About half a day, most like. We should be there by nightfall."

I thought about the captain, hunched over in the moonlight, watching the crew.

"At any rate, the captain wants to see you." She jerked her chin up at Safin. "Both of you."

I nodded and told Safin. He let out another cry of "Great treasure!" and scurried up my leg and settled around my neck, in his preferred traveling position. Together Hafsa and I walked to the captain's quarters. The crew's lassitude had worsened since the bells rang, and they called out to Hafsa as she walked past.

"Get some work done!" she shouted back at them, which only made them laugh. I was grateful they mostly ignored me.

Hafsa knocked on the captain's door. Rafi answered and gestured for us to step inside. It was as dimly lit as I remembered, and the air was thick and smelled of burning leaves.

Something shifted on the divan—the captain, stretched out on his back, smoking a pipe.

"I hear we've arrived," he said, and the smoke curled around him.

Rafi disappeared into the back room.

Safin leapt off my shoulder and landed on the floor with

a clank. The captain smiled at the noise and drew in another breath of smoke. When Safin scurried across the floor, the captain's eyes followed him.

"Great treasure!" Safin cried in Qilari.

"What did it say?"

"'Great treasure,'" I said.

"Ah, yes, the great treasure." The captain sat up. "Hafsa, you don't need to stay in here. Go make sure the crew actually steers us into the bay. They've been lazy these last few days."

"Yes, sir." Hafsa bowed her head and slipped out, a triangle of sunlight appearing and then disappearing with her.

The captain extinguished his pipe and set it on the table beside the divan. He stood and stretched, unfurling to his full height. Every time I saw him I thought he didn't look human, but I could not say why. All his parts were right, but they didn't come together in the right way.

"I want to know the directions before we disembark," he said, talking to me. "You will sit at that table there—" He pointed with his pipe "—and write down word for word what the little metal beastie has to say."

"Yes, sir."

He nodded and pointed at the table again. I told Safin what we needed to do. There was one chair set up at the table, and in front of that chair was a stack of parchment, a quill and ink.

"I'm assuming a nobleman's daughter knows how to write," the captain said.

I nodded, my throat too dried up to speak. I sat down at the table and dipped the quill in the ink. Safin hopped up on the table.

"I'm ready," I said.

"It's easy," Safin said, and I wrote that down, just to be sure. "But you will need small boats, not a big one like this. Follow the river away from the sea. Easy, easy!" He turned in an excited circle and blinked at me, eyes refracting in the lamplight.

I finished writing. "He's going to want more detail than that," I said. "How long do we follow the river?"

"A long time, yes. You will pass the bone trees and the baelfires. The great treasure lives in a house on the water. Most easy to spot."

I paused when he said *great treasure lives*. My Qilari had improved vastly over the last three months, and I didn't make the minor translation mistakes I did when I first started speaking with Safin. But it seemed odd to phrase it that way, to say *lives* instead of *is kept*. But then, Safin wasn't alive in the way I was. Maybe his understanding was different.

I finished writing out the instructions and handed them to the captain. He didn't say anything about the *great treasure lives*, only nodded like he was satisfied. He folded up the instructions and slipped them into the pocket of his jacket.

"These better guide us true." His gray eyes leered at me. "If they don't, I will kill that creature and then I will kill you."

I couldn't move. My body felt cold.

"You tell it what I just said." He gestured at Safin and turned away. I closed my eyes and took a deep breath and then relayed the message to Safin.

"Kill!" he said. "Oh no."

"You didn't lie to me, did you?"

"Of course not! I want to see the great treasure!"

"We're fine, then." I pressed my hand against my forehead. "We're fine."

But I couldn't shake the feeling that something was wrong.

⊗

WE TOOK FOUR BOATS TOTAL, a quarter of the crew. The full moon was a shining silver disk that lit the ocean with streaks of light. I rode in the head boat, with the captain and Rafi and Safin. Hafsa led the second boat, shouting orders as we bounced through the choppy waves.

"We can enter there," Safin said, and pointed. He was wrapped around my shoulders, close enough that I could hear his gears clicking.

I looked to where he pointed. The river mouth was narrow, flanked on either side by a pair of cypress trees with branches tangled overhead, forming an arch. The ocean was bright in the moonlight, but past that arch everything was dark.

"We can enter there," I said to the captain.

"I saw." He held my written instructions in his hand, and they rippled in the wind.

We passed through the cypress arch and the world went dark. No moonlight filtered through the thick vegetation of the swamp. The touched crewman scrambled to ignite lanterns, sending them up to drift alongside our boat. They cast small spheres of greenish light, hardly enough to see by. The air thickened with humidity. I stroked Safin's tail without thinking, and a noise rattled deep inside his chest, like a cat's purr.

We continued on. I relieved Rafi from rowing duty, and the rhythmic thump of the oars against the water soothed my nerves. No one spoke. We all seemed to be holding our breaths.

We came to a knot of white trees, twisting out of the swampy muck.

"The bone trees," Safin said.

I'd seen pictures of them in my illustrated history, but I'd always thought the pictures were an exaggeration. But here in the darkness, I saw they weren't. The bone trees looked like hands, with long thin fingers grasping the air. I knew from my book that if you cut them, they do not bleed sap, but dry white dust.

The captain's shoulders tensed as we slid past, and he kept his eyes on the bone trees, his hand on his pistol. Rafi lay a hand on the captain's upper arm, and for a moment the captain seemed to calm. Rafi dropped his hand, but I still saw it, that flicker of intimacy.

We passed the trees without incident.

"Now for the baelfires," the captain said.

"And then the treasure," I added.

"For your sake, I certainly hope so."

I'd read about the baelfires too, and I knew they were spots of light that lured weary travelers into the darkness. We rowed along, and the air shifted. My skin prickled, and Safin pressed closer to me.

A light blinked out in the trees.

"Concentrate," the captain said sharply. "Stay in the boat."

"Stay in the boats!" Rafi shouted, cupping his hand around his mouth. "Pass word along, Hafsa! Stay in the boats!"

Hafsa's voice echoed through the swamp, and then the next boat leader's, and the next. There were more baelfires now, bobbing out of the woods and over the water. They were lights, no different from our lanterns, but I wanted nothing more than to leap out of the boat and chase after one. I wanted to capture it and hold it in my hand. It would lead me to *her*, I knew it—it would lead me away from Qilar, away from the *Ocean's Dagger*, back to my home.

"Stay strong," Safin whispered. "They lie."

"They don't talk," I snapped.

"They still lie."

I plunged the oar into the water. The captain gazed after the baelfires, his face full of longing. It mirrored my own feelings, my own desire to leap into the water, to chase them through the darkness.

Rafi grabbed the captain's hand and squeezed it tight.

"Look," Safin said. "Look at their hands." His voice was urgent. I looked and it wasn't the captain and the first mate holding hands, but me and *her*. The baelfires might have claimed that they could take me to her, but she was the one who held me in place, the one who kept me safe.

I didn't think our trip through the baelfires would ever end. They flooded the swamp with light, but I rowed forward, sweat pouring down my back.

And then they blinked out and were gone.

"Is that the house?" the captain asked.

I jerked my head up. A house had formed in the sudden darkness, with white-washed walls and lights in the windows. It perched on the edge of the water, and lanterns —true lanterns and not baelfires—lit a path from the river to the door.

"The great treasure!" cried Safin.

"It's the house," I said, weariness dragging down the edges of my voice.

Safin slithered down my leg and rushed to the edge of the boat, curling his claws around the side. His eyes glowed.

"Yes!" he clattered. "Yes yes yes!"

The captain nodded at Rafi, who stood up and shouted for the boats' leaders to tie off at the rickety pier jutting over the river.

The captain climbed ashore and turned to face his men. "Rafi, Marjani, Hafsa, come with me. The rest of you wait for Hafsa's signal."

Hafsa nodded.

I crawled out of the boat, aware of intelligences passing through the trees, watching us, waiting. It was the first time I'd been on land for almost half a year, and my legs wobbled and shook. Hafsa caught me, and said in a strained voice, "You'll adjust."

"This way!" Safin shouted. "The great treasure will be delighted to see me!"

Another mistranslation. I was tired, and frightened, and I missed my life back in Jokja. But on shaking legs I followed the captain as he made his way up the house's front steps. The lanterns bobbed alongside us, winking like the baelfires. I trembled.

We came to the front door. Safin stood up on his hind legs, twisted the doorknob with his little clawed hands, and scurried inside.

"Great treasure!" he shouted.

Magic seeped out of the house, strong enough that I could feel it wrapping around me, thick and warm and heavier than the air. I was wary of crossing the threshold, and the others held back too, even the captain. Through the doorway, I saw no great treasure, only a small room with a lit hearth, shelves of books and trinkets, and an old woman sitting in a rocking chair.

"My life's light," she gasped in Qilari, rising to her feet. I don't think she even saw us as Safin scrambled up her skirts and wrapped around her neck as he'd done with me so many times before.

"The hell is this?" the captain roared, shoving us aside. "Where's the treasure?"

The woman glared at him. "A long way from the Empire," she said, not in Qilari but Empire, in the dialect of the aristocrats.

"I'm from no country," the captain said.

The woman glared at him for a moment longer. Then she gasped. "You're from the Mists," she said, and the magic intensified. I could smell it now, a scent like rotting flower petals.

The captain drew back and pulled out his pistol. "Not anymore. Where's the great treasure the automaton promised us?"

The woman curled her hands into fists. She didn't look away. Safin tightened around her shoulders, his eyes wide.

The great treasure lives.

The great treasure will be happy to see me.

I bent over and vomited. Hafsa shouted and jumped back. She asked me what was wrong. I ignored her, only wiping my mouth and looking up at Safin.

"Great treasure," I said in Qilari. "That's what you call her, isn't it? Great treasure."

"She is my great treasure, yes." Safin nodded his head. "She created me."

I thought I might faint.

"What the hell is going on!" the captain shouted. "What are you saying?"

The woman began to laugh. I could only stare at her, terror eating me from the inside. "Oh, you poor thing," she said in Qilari. "You told a man from the Mists you had a great treasure, and then you brought him to me." She laughed again. Her magic rippled, and the captain cursed and rubbed at his head.

They were going to kill me. I didn't know what the Mists was, but I knew they were pirates, and they were going to kill me.

The captain swung his pistol over to me. "What did she just say?"

"I'm the great treasure," the woman said, speaking Empire. "My name's Talia of the swamp, and I'm the only treasure you'll find here."

All I could see were the captain's horrible gray eyes. "I swear I didn't know!" I cried. "Safin never specified. I—" Tears formed in my lashes. The day I'd learned I was banished I'd felt like dying, but I didn't know what death was.

Ilafsa rested her hand on my back. She looked at the captain. I was aware of her hand hovering over her own pistol.

But the captain didn't shoot me. He stalked up to Talia and yanked Safin off her shoulder by the tail. Safin shrieked in protest and swung his tiny clawed hands at the captain's face. Talia shouted something in a language I didn't recognize, and the captain doubled over, dropping Safin to the floor. Safin landed on his feet and scrambled back to Talia.

The captain peered up at Talia. His face was pale and drawn. "So you're telling me you have the gold and the jewels to create that *thing* but there's no treasure in your home?"

"I used it all up." Talia smiled. "And besides, I said no treasure for *you*. I'm not in the habit of helping monsters."

"I'm not a monster." The captain straightened, although his steps were wobbling and uncertain. "I was cursed away from sunlight because I once helped you people. I'm never allowed back home. Don't talk to me about monsters."

Talia didn't seem like she believed him. I was still weeping, tears streaming silently over my face. Hafsa was the only one who noticed.

"If you want treasure so badly," Talia taunted, "you could always take Safin."

The captain glared at her. Safin coiled around her feet, but he didn't seem frightened. If the thought of absconding with Safin had crossed the captain's mind earlier, I doubted he would attempt it now, not with Talia's magic moving so thick and clammy though the little room.

"So that's it, then," the captain said. "You've got nothing." He turned to me. "Nothing," he spat. He pointed his pistol at me again.

I didn't want to die. Not yet.

"Wait!" I shouted through my tears. Everyone looked at me, and my thoughts churned to keep up. "What about—what about a reward?"

"Excuse me?" Talia said.

I rubbed my sleeve over my face to dry my eyes. I drew myself up like I was still my father's daughter. "A reward. For bringing back Safin."

The captain lowered his pistol.

"He clearly wanted to come back. I'm not sure why he was on the *Ocean's Rose—*"

"He was stolen." Talia lifted her chin. "By pirates like you."

"The *Ocean's Rose* was a passenger liner," I said. "It was overtaken by pirates later. Whoever stole him wasn't a pirate."

Talia didn't say anything.

"So, yes, he was stolen." I took a deep breath, trying to steady my heartbeat. "But not by us. We brought him back to you. How many people, pirate or otherwise, would have done that? It would have been easy to sail on to Lisirra and have him smashed to pieces for the gold."

Safin blinked up at me.

"But we didn't. We returned him."

"Because you thought there was a real treasure."

"We still returned him."

I was desperate, but Talia looked at me for a long time, like she was sizing me up. Then Safin slid up her skirts and whispered something in her ear. She looked at him, looked back to me.

"Fine," she finally said. "Pick something off the shelves. Bottom ones only."

I felt dizzy. Maybe I wouldn't die today after all.

I crouched down in front of the bottom shelves. It was crowded with charms and spells and potions. Magic. I didn't recognize what sort, whether earth magic or water magic or wind magic, because I'd never really had the capacity for enchantment. But I did recognize that these charms were simple. Basic. The touched crewman could put them together without even trying.

I glanced over at the captain. His gun was still out, and he was glaring at me through his stringy hair.

I decided to take a chance.

"These are worth nothing." I rose to my feet. "We sailed three months to bring Safin back to you, and he's not even injured. Not missing a single scale. Surely you can part with something a little more powerful than a half-day protection charm."

Talia grinned. "So you aren't as stupid as you look. Fine. Choose from any shelf."

I turned back to the shelves. Most of the other items were too advanced for me, so I gestured Hafsa over.

"Those bags there," she said. "They're excellent for navigation and evading enemies. Most of this wouldn't do us any good, but those—those will do nicely."

I grabbed the bags off the shelf. They were sewn out of worn velvet and felt empty.

Talia scoffed at our choice. "Sailors," she muttered. "*Pirates.*"

"Thank you," I told her. "For the reward."

I didn't expect her to respond, but instead she spoke in Qilari: "You watch out for that captain. He's not human."

I didn't know what to say to that. Rafi and Hafsa and the captain had already stepped outside. A few more days and I'd be in Idai City. Maybe the captain wasn't human. I don't think it mattered to his crew, not one bit.

"Goodbye, Safin," I said, "I'm glad you found your great treasure."

And then I stepped back out into the thick night. The boats were waiting.

Jokja was gone. *She* was gone. But I was ready to find my way to a new home.

The End

The Witch's Betrayal

When I stepped out of the shadows, the scent of night-blooming flowers overwhelmed me. I wasn't expecting a garden, not this far into the desert, and the sight of it put me on edge. Everything about this commission suggested it was simple, routine—but these flowers spoke of magic.

I did not want to deal with magic tonight. I wasn't *supposed* to deal with magic tonight.

I threaded through the garden, coasting on the backs of shadows, the metallic taste of the tracking spell lingering in my throat. The house loomed up ahead, wrapped in heavy ropes of jasmine. It was a simple house, white clay glowing in the moonlight, and it had been simple to track the target here. Simple, as I said. Routine.

The windows were dark, no candles or magic-cast lanterns illuminating the night. Good: the thick shadows made my magic easier. I dissolved into darkness, sliding away from the garden and the scent of flowers and the cold night air. The darkness was a different sort of cold— death-cold, a friend at the Order always said, and I knew what he meant, because of the way the shadows curl into your nose and mouth and lungs, as if to drown you. But I didn't mind. That drowning cold meant I was hidden. Protected. It meant I could watch unseen from the places people did not look.

I passed through the walls of the house.

I pulled myself out of the darkness.

Something was wrong.

I stopped, half-in, half-out. The air was charged, crackling with residual magic. Through the haze, I saw that the garden was not confined to the outside of the house. Shrubs emerged out of the slats in the floorboards, vines grew along the walls, palm fronds hung from the ceiling beams. Every plant was heavy with blossoms, and I could make out the scent of them, heady and unnatural.

Too much magic in too short a time. No one ever intended these plants to grow here, but the magic transformed the house so completely that they did anyway. They were a side-effect, a dangerous one.

Fallout, we called it in the Order.

By instinct, I sank back into the shadows and emerged a safe distance from the house, in the dry desert sands. The house and its garden rippled in the night wind. I took a deep breath, steadying myself. The fallout hadn't begun to affect me, not in that short a time, but no human could stay in that house for long without transforming with the magic. Fallout's nature was such that it could never be controlled. Not even by someone like me.

I retreated into Kajjil, the Order's secret space between worlds, and cast the tracking spell again. I found my target immediately: he was in the house, still alive and still human.

This wasn't right. If he was in the house, the magic would have subsumed him. If the magic had subsumed him, I would not have been able to track him with my spell.

I cast it again and received the same results. Frustrated, I stepped out of Kajjil and stood in the wind and tried to decide what to do next. My first thought was that this was someone from the Order, a rival, hoping to ruin my commission – that sort of thing happens frequently enough that it was worth the consideration. But the magic in the house was not ack'mora. More likely, the target had received word that was I coming and had escaped— although I didn't know how he could have heard, or what magic might have confused my tracking spell.

The wind picked up, blowing from the direction of the house and bringing with it the scent of the garden, the scent of living magic. I couldn't leave, not with my commission incomplete. When I am given a target, they must be eradicated. I have no say in the matter. Ever since I was a little boy taken away from his mother, my actions have belonged to the Order, and I've learned, over the years, to accept it.

But if I wanted any hope of finding this target, I would need something, some *clue,* as to how he had evaded me.

I traveled through the shadows. When I was back inside the house, I did not emerge completely, though it was difficult to see. Going inside was dangerous, but I could not go back to the Order empty-handed. Flowers crowded the rooms. The fallout tugged at the edges of the shadows, trying to draw me out. I didn't let it. I worked quickly, moving from room to room. The fallout made things confusing, difficult to latch on to.

And then I found something.

The highest concentration of magic was located in the bedroom. It was so dense and unstable that I didn't dare move beyond the doorway, not even half-wrapped in shadow. But I didn't need to go further to recognize the eerie, glowing white flowers twining around the bed. They were a particular flower, bred by a particular woman. I had seen similar flowers as seedlings. I had walked through a garden of such flowers, side by side with the woman who had grown them.

"Leila," I said, and the shadows took me away.

⚜

I RAPPED on Leila's door. She didn't answer. I shouted her name and rapped harder, the door banging in its frame. Still no answer. A discouraging sign.

I stepped away from the door, turned and looked at the empty street. A magic-cast lantern flickered overhead, casting eerie golden-limned shadows along the rows of houses. Despite being in the city, the air here was clean and bright in comparison to the magic-soaked air surrounding the target's house, and I breathed it in, trying to clear my head after the journey through Kajjil.

The stillness settled around me. I turned back to Leila's house and pulled out my sword, banging on the door with its hilt. The sound echoed up and down the street. "Leila!" I shouted. "Let me in!"

A light flickered on in one of the nearby houses. I cursed and sheathed my sword, melting into the shadows. I didn't want to enter Leila's house without permission. That's something I only do with targets. But I couldn't wait.

When no one came onto the street, I stuck out my foot and kicked her door one last time for good measure. And only then did it slide open, pale light spilling across her porch, illuminating the flowers she grew in ceramic pots, the same ones I'd seen at the target's house.

Her face appeared, beautiful in the moonlight. Her hair curled around her bare shoulders and her eyes were lined with that dark, smoky make-up she wore when she wanted something. It was clear she had not been asleep.

"Oh, well, isn't this a shame?" she called out, peering into the street. "I was certain it was my dear friend Naji at the door, but I don't see anyone here." She pouted. "I guess I'll have to go back inside."

She began to pull her door closed. I stuck my foot out again and it jarred to a stop.

"You know I'm here," I said softly.

Leila turned in the direction of my voice and gazed at a space over my left shoulder. She smiled wickedly, her eyes glinting.

"I can't *see* you," she said.

Leila always made me nervous, despite my fondness for her. She was not a woman to be charmed by a simple smile, and so hiding myself was one of my ways of keeping the upper hand.

"But you know I'm here." I moved closer to her, staying on the edges of the light. The shadows drifted across her face, and she closed her eyes, and smiled again.

"But I can't see you," she said. "How do I know I'm not simply going mad? This could all be a dream."

"You don't expect me to believe you were asleep."

Something flickered in her expression. I caught it because I was looking for it.

"And what do you think I was doing?"

I emerged then, stepping into the light spilling out of her house. She leaned up against her doorframe and watched me.

"There you are," she said, trailing one hand along my cheek, just as my shadows had done to her. "Always a joy to see your face, Naji."

"May I come in?"

"Of course." She held the door open. I could smell the steely scent of river water coming from inside her house, the scent that followed her everywhere. She was saving her money, I knew, in order to move to a new house in the canyon, close to the river where her power would be strongest.

I went inside, and she shut the door behind us.

"So you're feeling lonely tonight?" she asked, sliding up close to me, slipping her arm in mine. I let her, of course. "Couldn't stand the thought of spending the evening with only those dusty old books?"

"I had a commission."

Her arm stiffened.

"Did you? I take it that it went well, if you're here for a celebratory tumble." She laughed.

I forced myself to ignore her, to not think about the unraveling magic of her touch. "You know it didn't."

"Didn't what?"

"Didn't go well!" I pulled away from her. She blinked up at me, her face guileless. "The target was gone before I got there."

"Are you sure you should be telling me that? I don't think the Order would be glad to know that you let someone beat you to the job--"

"I didn't say he was dead. I said he wasn't there."

She didn't say anything. Her hair fell across her left eye in a way that made me want to push it aside. I didn't.

"The house was drowning in fallout."

"Sounds like he got away, then."

"Someone helped him."

"Oh, Naji, I know it may be hard for you Jadorr'a to understand, but there *are* people in the Empire with more power than--"

"I saw your damned river flowers all over the place."

She stopped, lifting her chin a little, draping herself against the wall. Her expression changed. It was no longer guileless at all.

"I was hoping they wouldn't send you," she said.

"Where is he?"

She watched me for a few moments without answering. I returned her gaze.

"Did you really think it'd be that easy? That you'd ask and I'd tell you?"

"Darkest night, Leila! I can't go back to the Order unless the commission is completed! This was supposed to be *routine.*"

"So stay here with me." She slid forward and reached out for me. I jerked away from her.

"Where is he?" I asked again, although I knew it was futile trying to intimidate Leila.

She slumped back and sighed. For a moment she looked older than she really was. Ancient. The sight chilled me.

"What made you think this would be simple?" she asked.

"What?"

"This commission. You said it was supposed to be routine. Why would you think that?"

"I didn't think *you* were going to be involved, for one thing."

Leila narrowed her eyes. "You should never assume that, Naji. And you should never assume a commission is going to be *routine*."

"Don't tell me how to do my job."

She put her hand on my shoulder. "I really didn't think they'd give him to you." Her voice was soft and stripped bare. I knew she meant it.

"Why not?"

"Because you're young." She looked up at me, her eyes big and luminous. In other circumstances, I would have kissed her and finished our conversation in the morning. But not tonight. "Because he's a dangerous man."

"Most people would say I'm a dangerous man."

Leila's face broke open in a smile. Everything about her transformed. "Ah, true enough. But you don't like to hurt people, and he does."

"So why'd you hide him?"

"He paid me." She shrugged. "I've almost got enough to move out of the city." And then she stepped away and I could feel the negative space of her absence. She didn't look at me.

"Fine," I said. "You hid him. You did what he paid you for. I'm assuming he only paid you to hide him once? If the Jadorr'a come after him a second time--"

She looked at me over her shoulder. "Don't," she said, her voice dark. "I told you, he's dangerous. You're in over your head. Go back to the Order and tell them to send someone else."

"I can't do that."

She rolled her eyes and swirled away from me. "You

won't be able to find him. I know too much about your tracking spells."

"There are other ways to track someone."

She stopped. Her hand traced along her thigh and her hip, a distracted gesture.

"Leila," I said. "If you're waiting for the rest of his payment, you know I can get that for you."

She didn't answer.

"I'll find him eventually."

Her shoulders hitched, and she looked at me again, her spine curving beneath the thin fabric of her dress. I couldn't look away from her.

She smiled sadly and said, "I'll be praying to the spirits of the river that you don't."

❦

AFTER I LEFT Leila's house I slipped through the shadows until I came to a bar on the edge of the city, one that was open despite the late hour. It was also completely empty, and the waiter watched me with alarm as I moved across the room and took a table in the corner, no doubt recognizing the dark robes and carved armor that branded me a member of the Order. That has always been the hardest part of being Jadorr'a. The way people look at you like you're a monster.

I stared at the waiter until he came over and took my order, and then I slouched back in my chair and drummed my fingers against the table. I was putting off communicating with the Order, to be sure, but I also wanted to consider the best way to track the target— Lisim Sarr. Without my magic, I would have to use his name.

I hated thinking on the names of my targets.

The waiter brought my drink, a slim glass of sugar wine imported from the south. I drank it fast enough that my head spun. I could feel the waiter cowering next to his stack of coffee cups even though I took pains not to look at him.

I supposed I should start by finding out who my target *was*.

I finished my sugar wine and gestured the waiter over. He picked up the empty glass with trembling hands. "Anything else, sir?"

I pulled out three sheets of pressed copper, twice what the wine cost. "Do you know anyone named Lisim Sarr?"

The waiter stared at me like he thought I was playing a trick.

"Well?" I asked. "Do you?"

"No, sir."

I studied his face carefully, but I saw no hint that he was lying. No matter. I hadn't expected things to go *that* easily.

"Ah, well," I told him. "Thank you anyway."

I pushed away from my table and walked out of the bar, leaving the waiter shivering in my wake. I needed an inn. It was ridiculous, that I should have to stay in an inn in my own city, but under no circumstances could I return to the Order's manor house unless my commission was complete. And so I traveled through the shadows to the pleasure district, where I would have to endure filthier rooms but fewer questions. I selected an inn close to the docks and requested a room that looked over the sea. The sea and the river aren't the same, of course, but the lapping of the waves reminded me of Leila.

After I paid for my room, I asked the innkeeper the same question I had asked the waiter at the bar.

"Sarr?" he said, caught unawares.

I nodded.

"No, I don't --" His eyes flicked away from me. "I'm afraid I haven't heard of him, no."

I leaned close and drew out the shadows enough that they crawled over the counter. The innkeeper stumbled backward.

"You shouldn't lie to me," I said.

"I ain't lying, honest— I've heard the name, but I don't— don't *know* him. Don't want to know him." He tossed the key at me. I caught it, and the shadows retreated into the light.

"Where have you heard the name?"

"Here and there, you know. The girls don't like him." He jerked his head in the direction of the street. "I always give 'em a free meal if they bring their business here, and I've heard 'em whispering."

"That's it? You've only heard his name from the street girls?"

"Nah, you hear it from others sometimes too. But I don't know nothing about him, I swear. It's just a name."

"Thank you for your cooperation," I said. This had turned out more useful than I might have expected, and it made sense that an innkeeper in the pleasure district would know of a dangerous man. If Sarr was indeed as dangerous as Leila was claiming.

Doubtful.

In my room, I locked the door, took off my armor and turned down the sheets on my shabby, creaking bed. I stood in the window and looked out over the ocean glimmering beneath the stars. I was wasting time in every way I could think of. But I knew I couldn't put off contacting the Order forever.

When I finally decided to get it over with, sunlight was

just beginning to creep up over the water. I fell away from the room, through shadows, through Kajjil, until I was a shade in the flickering firelight of the Order's assignment room. Zahir was waiting for me with a glass of dark red wine. Seeing him filled me with a dull, familiar dread that I did my best to ignore.

"This is taking longer than we expected, Naji."

I felt like I was a child again, being scolded for doing poorly in training.

"I encountered complications." My voice reverberated against my ears. My body was still in the inn, stretched out on the bed, surrounded by dawn's light and the scent of the sea, but my voice and thoughts, all the rest of me, were at the Order.

"Complications?"

I chose my words carefully. "Yes. Someone has helped him. He evaded my tracking spells."

Zahir said nothing.

"I'm confident I'll be able to track him."

"This was not meant to be an involved operation."

"And it won't be. It should be completed by tomorrow evening."

Zahir snorted into his glass. "Do you have any idea how many times 'tomorrow evening' becomes 'two months from now'?"

"I've already begun my investigation. I don't foresee it taking two months."

"Let's hope not." Zahir set his glass down and looked at me— looked at my shade. He seemed bored, sleepy, irritated. Which was fair: he was an old man. I imagine he didn't appreciate staying up all night waiting for me to bring word. "I'll give you until tomorrow's sunrise. If it takes any longer than that, expect punishment."

I shivered.

"Yes, of course. Thank you, Zahir."

He snorted again and waved me away. Five heartbeats later I was back in the inn room, weak gray sunlight filtering through the window.

Tomorrow's sunrise.

One full day.

I could find the most dangerous man in Lisirra in one full day.

⁂

I ONLY ALLOWED myself to sleep for four hours. When I woke up, the sunlight was a bright, sparkling mass choking out the air of my bedroom. It hurt my eyes. But I couldn't allow myself the luxury of sleep right now.

Before I left, I cast a tracking spell to double check. According to my magic, Sarr was still nestled safely in that house in the desert. I muttered a few profanities, directing them at Leila.

Then I set a ward on my room and went downstairs. The inn's main room was empty save for the innkeeper, who wouldn't look at me. Outside, the pleasure district was just beginning to stir. It was nearly noon. I bought a meat pie from a street vendor and ate it as I walked down the street, keeping my eyes out for street girls. Since the innkeeper had mentioned they sometimes spoke of Sarr, I thought they were the best place to begin my investigation.

Without magic, I would have to track Sarr through the trails all people leave, through his connections and relationships. And right now, the only relationship I had uncovered was with the girls who prowled the pleasure district's streets after dark, providing it with its name.

However, uncovering street girls during the middle of the day proved more difficult than I thought. I wound up at a dancehall after half an hour of wandering. It had only just opened, strings of magic-cast lanterns blinking red and blue and gold, washed out in the sunlight. I went in. Most of the tables were empty and the air was thick with pipe smoke. Magic jangled in the background, emanating from an unenthusiastic band in the corner. A few women danced onstage, looking as bored as the band.

A woman came to ask if I wanted anything to drink. She wore a spangled dress that caught the light and threw dots of color across the floor. Her eyes were made-up with same dark shades that Leila favored.

Like Leila, and unlike most people in the city, she didn't act frightened of me.

"I don't need anything to drink," I told her, making sure to smile, to put her at ease. "But I do need your help."

She looked at me warily.

"I'm looking for someone," I said. "Lisim Sarr."

Her eyes went wide when I said his name. She glanced over her shoulder, toward the door, then back to me. The music played on.

"Are you going to kill him?" she asked.

"What?"

"You're an assassin, aren't you? Is that why you're looking for him?" She slid into the chair next to me and put her hand on my arm, her touch feather-soft. I smiled at her again, and her eyes sparkled a little— with excitement, I thought. Interest.

"I'm not allowed to tell you that," I said.

"Then why are you looking for him? Do you want to help him?"

I hesitated. I really didn't like tracking people this way. It was too nuanced, too dependent on understanding the network of human connection. But I was astute enough to notice a flicker of fear when she asked if I wanted to help him.

My being Jadorr'a, that didn't scare her. But the thought that I might be helping Sarr --

"No," I said. "I just need to talk to him."

"You won't be able to. He's mad." She pulled her hand away from me and slouched in her chair. Her hair fell across her face. The band finished their song and desultory applause scattered across the room. The woman picked her head up a little. "That's what everyone says, anyway. And he's wicked as well. Although isn't that what you're supposed to do? Kill wicked men?"

Her words surprised me. I regarded her for a moment. There aren't many people in the Empire who understand the history of the Order, who understand that we were formed long ago to keep the people of the desertlands safe from kings would rather rage war with each other than rule. Most only know us as the killers for hire that we've become, and not for what we are supposed to be.

Of course, we had never exactly been vigilantes hunting down all the wickedness in the desert, but the notion was close enough.

"Yes," I said.

"Then you should kill Sarr. He's the wickedest man in Lisirra." She pushed her hair away from her face and looked up at the stage. A new song had begun, slow and slippery and sad, and the dancer writhed in the smoky blue light. "I'm not just a waitress. Or a dancer. I own this place." She glanced at me. "I don't normally take drink orders, but my daytime waitress is dead. He killed her."

"How do you know it was him?"

"The whispers." She paused, then explained. "The girls, the ones who work at night, they bring us information. Who's dangerous, who isn't, that sort of thing. We call it the whispers." Silence. "He uses his victims to work magic. He does different things to them. With my waitress, he took out all her insides and filled her with stones from the desert. For a spell. They wouldn't tell me what it did."

I didn't say anything, but I felt a tightness in my chest, that Leila had helped someone like this.

"The thing about Sarr," she went on, "is that he's powerful, powerful enough to change his appearance. So you can't go by that. It's always the powerful ones who are the cruelest." She sighed. "You're not going to kill him. Someone has to hire you, isn't that how it works? And who would hire the assassins to come kill someone terrorizing the pleasure district girls?"

She said this all matter-of-factly, a resigned fierceness in her features.

"I can't talk about it," I said. "I'm sorry."

She watched me across the table. Then she touched my arm again, her fingers grazing across my skin.

"I've no idea where to find him," she said, "but the whispers say he used to work with Naim Ajeeri. Do you know who that is?"

I shook my head.

"He runs the night market here. Another wizard." She shrugged. "He's mad, too, but in a different way. He might be able to help you. He lives in an apartment down by the sea. It's easy to find. The walls are white but the door is painted bright red."

"Thank you." I pulled out a handful of pressed silver and laid it on the table. The woman stared at the silver for a few moments; then she covered it with her hand. When she slid her hand away from the table, it was gone.

She looked up at me. "You're not how I pictured an assassin."

"Is that so?"

"You're younger. And more handsome." She stood up. She moved like liquid in the ashy light.

"If you kill him," she said, "come back and tell me."

৩৩৩

THE WOMAN at the dancehall was correct; it was easy to find Ajeeri's apartment building. It stretched down half the street, the white paint flaking off and lying like ashes in the surrounding gardens, which were dry and desiccated from the sun. No one to care for them, I supposed.

What wasn't so easy was finding Ajeeri's particular apartment. I made my way inside the building easily enough, traveling through the shadows until I emerged in the narrow, dusty hallway. Voices seeped through the walls. Each door was dark and narrow and marked with painted-on numbers. But I had no way of knowing which belonged to him.

I slipped back outside and found a quiet alley in which to retreat into Kajjil and cast the tracking spell. It was difficult with only a name, but he was close by, in his apartment.

I uncovered him easily, hiding away on the apartment building's top floor.

I left Kajjil but did not return fully to the world. For a moment I hovered amidst the cool damp shadows, trying to decide if I should go to his front door or if I should slip directly into his apartment. He wasn't a target, technically, but I also didn't want to drag my investigation out any further than was necessary.

When I stepped out of darkness, I stepped into the middle of his living room.

It was empty, dark, cool. Thick brocaded curtains hung unmoving in front of the windows. The room, the entire apartment, had that still quality I associate with nighttime, with a house full of sleep and dreams.

Of course. He ran the night market. Why would he be awake during the day?

I slipped through the labyrinthine hallway, opening every door I came across. The apartment was full of the curiosities of a night market— clumps of rare flowers drying from the rafters, shelves of glass candles and spirit paintings, stacks of spellbooks. It didn't take me long to find Ajeeri, though. He was asleep, as I'd expected, sprawled out on his stomach on top of the sheets of his bed, snoring a little. For a moment I hovered in the doorway of the room, watching him in the dark. Appraising him. He was wiry and thin, his hair going patchy at the back of his head.

I stepped one foot into the room.

Ajeeri sat straight up, his eyes wide open. I pulled my sword by reflex. His gaze zeroed in on me and for a moment he just sat in the bed, sheets crumpled around his waist, watching me.

Then he bounded off the bed, running in long quick

strides toward the window.

"Stop!" I roared, drawing my sword across my palm and pulling magic from deep inside me, casting a web of it over the apartment. Ajeeri slammed into the magic shield and fell flat on his back. I moved with the shadows until I was crouched over him, sword at his throat.

"This isn't right!" he babbled. "Do I look like a threat to the Empire? I just run a night market, that's all. I provide a service to the city of Lisirra --"

"I'm not here to kill you." I hauled him up and tossed him on the bed, although I kept my sword out, more as an intimidation tactic than anything else. My magic still crackled in the air and my blood was smeared across my palm, the wound stinging. Ajeeri looked around the room, his eyes bright. Trying to find a weakness in the magic, no doubt. I strengthened it.

"What do you want?" he asked, his eyes finally settling on me. "You say you're not here to kill me, yet you trap me in my own bed." He lifted his hands halfway to his head, as if they were shackled in invisible chains. "*Blood magic.*" He spat the words out, the way most people do.

"I'm looking for Lisim Sarr."

Ajeeri went still. The frantic expression left his face.

I stepped toward him.

"I'm afraid I don't know a Lisim. Or a Sarr."

He'd gone too long without answering, and he was too glib, and I could smell the lie souring in the wave of magic.

"Don't lie to me." I lifted my sword. He turned his head and flinched a little but otherwise didn't move. "I heard you used to be partners."

"I've never had a partner. Do you know anything about me, assassin? Ask anyone in the pleasure district and they'll tell you what I always say: a partner's not worth the trouble. He'll take half and leave you when you need --"

I leapt onto him, digging one knee into his chest bone, pressing him back into the bed. He squawked and struggled to free himself until I held the sword at his throat.

"I heard," I said, "that you used to be partners."

Ajeeri stared at me. He didn't look frightened, exactly, only cautious, careful. I pressed the flat side of my sword against his neck. The heat from his skin clouded the metal.

"Who told you that?" Ajeeri asked.

I didn't answer him.

"Partners isn't the right word."

I waited for him to say more, but he only stared at me over the curve of the sword.

"So you do know him," I said.

"Everyone knows him. Everyone down here, in this charming piece of the city." He wriggled beneath me. "Do you think you could get up? Your knee's causing me a bit of pain— "

"No. Why isn't partners the right word?"

"Because we weren't bloody partners. Why are you asking after him?"

I didn't say anything.

"You want to recruit him, is that it? He'd be good for your sort, I imagine, the sort of things he's done. I hear the assassins are always looking for the cruelest killers."

I hit Ajeeri in the nose, a short sharp jab. I did it without thinking. Blood flowed over his mouth and I added its strength, its life's light, to the magic already shimmering in his apartment.

"Curse you," he muttered.

"I don't kill dancing girls," I said.

Ajeeri glared at me over his smeared blood. "Not just dancing girls he's killed. Anyone he can find down here. Sailors, children..."

I thought of Leila. *I almost have enough money to move out of the city.* She knew who she'd helped. She'd called him a dangerous man. I felt vaguely sick. My magic rippled with spots of weakness.

Focus.

"If you weren't partners, what were you?"

Ajeeri sighed. "I mentored him, for a while. Taught him a bit of city magic. I'd the intention of letting him take over the night market when I couldn't stand it anymore. But he had a streak of darkness in him. Some people do. I should have recognized it earlier, but he was charming enough that it was difficult to see." Ajeeri paused and stared up at the ceiling. "It's not a good combination with city magic, that darkness. The worst parts of the city'll get under your skin and bring out the worst parts of you. That's what happened to him."

I eased my knee off his chest but kept the sword at his throat.

"Why does he kill people?"

I hadn't meant to ask it. I didn't need to know his reasons. I only needed to know where to find him.

Ajeeri looked at me. "I don't know," he said. "You're the killer here. You tell me."

My magic trembled. Ajeeri grinned, white teeth against red blood. The sight of it was enough for me to regain my focus.

"Where is he?" I said, pressing the sword more firmly against his neck.

"I don't know!"

I tilted the sword, enough that he'd feel the pressure of the blade but not enough to cut him too deeply. A few drops of blood appeared. My magic swelled.

"I don't know! I don't keep in contact with a man like that. You want to find him, follow the damned bodies. We've gone a few weeks without one. It's won't be long, I'm sure."

I pulled away from him, leaving him sprawled on the bed. He lifted his head a little. My magic coruscated around us.

He was telling the truth.

OUTSIDE OF AJEERI'S APARTMENT, the sun was blinding, bouncing off the white walls of the houses and the far-off sparkle of the sea. For a moment it seemed like all the shadows had been wiped away, and I felt alone and vulnerable.

I walked to Leila's house. I didn't intend to; I intended to make my way to the city's center, where I could access the hall of records to investigate the murders. To follow the damned bodies, as Ajeeri had said. But I didn't have time, and after speaking to the woman in the dancehall, I didn't want to read about his murders anyway. I could imagine the sort of things darkness might draw out of a man like that. What abominations he'd create out of the magic of sacrifice.

Leila's house was closed up tight against the afternoon sun. I hadn't bothered to shift into the shadows on my way there, and I was soaked in sweat, my hair sticking to the side of my face. Penance, I suppose, for being what I am, for being something so close to Sarr. Blood magic is a sort of darkness. Maybe not the same, but close enough.

I banged on Leila's door until she answered. When she saw me standing on her porch, she didn't say anything, only held the door open for me. I went inside and stripped off my armor and collapsed on the divan she kept in her main room. She brought me water in a simple wooden cup. I drank it down. She sat down on the divan beside me and tangled her fingers up in my hair.

"Why did you walk here?" she asked.

"Why did you help Sarr?"

Her hand froze against the crown of my head. Silence swallowed us both.

"I told you not to track him," she whispered.

I sat up, pulling away from her. She didn't reach for me.

"Why did you help him?"

"I explained that to you."

"You knew what he did. You had to, if you were warning me away from him --"

She looked away.

"Did you?" I said. "Did you know?"

She lifted her head and stared at a point in the distance. Sunlight poured around her, casting her skin in a soft golden glow. "Of course I knew," she said softly. "I didn't think they'd send you." She paused. "You shouldn't go after him anyway. Take the punishment from the Order and tell them to send someone else."

"This isn't about me being in danger!" I stood up, anger pumping through me. "You know how few times I get to do something— something *worthwhile*? That my work can keep people safe?"

She didn't answer.

"I'm not completing the commission merely so I can avoid punishment. I don't know why you'd even think that."

I could hardly look at her. The past three years I'd spent my life running errands for the rich, because that was what the Order had become. Now Leila had stripped me of an opportunity to save the lives of people in the pleasure district, dancing girls and children. All so she could have a little taste of wealth herself.

"You disgust me," I told her.

She looked at me, then, and I was startled to see she was crying. I'd never seen Leila cry. I didn't think she was capable of it.

"What was I supposed to do?" she asked. "If I hadn't taken his offer it would be another four years before I could move. I'm *dying* here, Naji. Literally. I need the river."

I stalked away from her, heat rising up in my veins. "You have the money," I snapped. "Just tell me where he is."

"I don't *know*."

I stopped, staring at her door.

"I cast the spell, but he drew up his own magic at the last minute and it wiped my memory clean. I have no idea where I sent him. That's why I didn't tell you earlier."

The room wrapped around us.

"I'm never going to find him, am I?" I said.

"Not asking after him. It won't work. He's got my magic and his, and I can't undo my own spell. I don't even remember what I cast. He took it all away."

I continued staring at her door, my thoughts heavy. I had the afternoon; I had the nighttime. And then the Order would punish me, and I would have let a murderer go free.

The thought twisted me up.

"I'm sorry," Leila said behind me, "But there's nothing --"

I turned to face her. "Can I borrow one of your rooms?"

"What?"

"One of your rooms. Can I use it safely? I need to slip away."

She stared at me like she didn't understand. "I told you, it's impossible --"

"Darkest night, Leila, just answer my question."

She sighed and fell back on the divan. "Of course you can use one of my rooms," she said, and she wiped the tears away from her eyes.

I didn't say anything, only followed the familiar path of her hallway. There was a room tucked away in the back of her house that I thought would serve my purposes well. A closet, really, with no windows and no chances of distraction. I put up a locking charm when I went in—a precaution, although I didn't expect Leila to interrupt.

I traced my knife along the edges of the Order tattoos, dropping the blood on Leila's floor in a lopsided circle. I didn't have all the supplies to do this properly, but I hoped my blood and my urgency would be enough for me to find the answers I needed. I tossed my knife aside, out of the circle, and sat down and began to chant in the language of the Jadorr'a, the words low and rough in the back of my throat. Magic steamed in the air.

I fell away.

My body stayed in Leila's house but *I* opened my eyes in the center of Kajjil. When I joined the Order as a little boy, I memorized spell after spell, but this one, this opening of a gateway, was the first.

This was the part of Kajjil that held answers.

Kajjil's center looks different to every individual. For me it was a desert of glass. The wind sounded like chimes. I wandered over the landscape, murmuring my question in the language of the Jadorr'a:

How do I find Lisim Sarr? How do I find Lisim Sarr?

I wasn't sure I would get an answer. The wind slipped through the glass dunes. My feet ached. My eyes watered.

How do I find Lisim Sarr? I asked, raising my voice.

And then Kajjil's center answered. The place was created by the Order years and years ago, and they built it out of the knowledge of every Jadorr'a who had ever been. Those Jadorr'a answered me now, whispering on the wind:

Fire.

Fire.

Fire.

"Fire?" I didn't understand. I've no capacity for fire magic.

Fire, the voice said, rising in a clamor. *Fire fire firefire-firefire.*

And then flames erupted out of the glass ahead of me, golden flames shot through with human bodies, and I understood.

The Fire of Amkarja.

The flames extinguished in a curl of smoke, but the voices continued to chant *fire* as I stood in Kajjil, afraid to return to my body. I knew, in theory, how to ignite the Fire. It was one of the spells I had memorized as a little boy. A spell my tutor had warned me away from.

"To find what is lost," he'd said, leaning over me as I worked. "It never goes out. It will always keep looking. But there are easier ways to track a target."

And he was right, assuming the commission was simple. Routine.

I pulled away from Kajjil and reconnected with my body. For a moment I lay in the circle and stared up at the ceiling. The room was darker than when I had left, no bright sunlight peeking through the crack in the door. I was losing time.

I stood up, gathered my knife, and crept out to Leila's hallway. Her house was empty, still, and dark. I found her sleeping on the divan, the skin around her eyes red from crying. I knelt down beside her and shook her awake. She gasped a little and her eyes opened and gave me a long sad look.

"I'm sorry," she said.

"You aren't a very good person," I said.

"I know. I'm all right with it." She reached over and cupped my face in her hand and smiled. Her touch was gentle and soft and it reminded me of every other time she had ever touched me. Stupid as it was, I couldn't stay angry with her. "You're not, though," she said. "Not finding him won't change that."

"I know how to find him." I took her hand in mine and squeezed. She watched me, her expression unreadable. I stood up. "I saw the way in Kajjil."

She pushed herself up onto one arm. "Are you going to do something stupid?"

"I'm going to stop him."

"So yes."

I turned away from her and walked to the door. Behind me, she said my name. She told me to wait.

But I ignored her.

I WENT INTO THE DESERT, far away from the lights of the city. It was darker than I could have imagined, so dark I could barely see my own hands. I cast a handful of small lanterns, and they floated around my head like wayward stars, illuminating everything with pale blue light. They didn't help much.

I'd been able to procure a stack of firewood from a desert tree growing outside the city wall. With my magic I cut the tree into pieces and shoved them into a burlap sack I stole from Leila's house, along with a bit of flint from the pile beside her stove, and here I was, with everything I needed to cast the Fire of Amkarja. A stack of wood, a piece of flint, and my own blood.

I began to work, slowly and methodically. I arranged the firewood in a circle, making a neat, even pile. Putting off the inevitable. When I was finished I stepped back, my arms crossed over my chest. It was cold without the sun, and I shivered beneath my armor and my robes, although I wasn't sure I was shivering from the cold.

I knew how the fire was supposed to work: I would cast it, using my theoretical knowledge, and the magic would draw me in close, making me a part of the fire. The flames would show me the faces of those who were lost. I would ask the fire to show me Lisim Sarr. Because I am Jadorr'a, and because I gave a part of myself up, it would comply, although I knew I would have to be careful, I would have to be polite. Armed with this new information, I could travel through the shadows to kill Sarr in his bed, completing my commission and saving the lives of the people in the pleasure district.

Once it was done, I would need to ask the Order to send help to extinguish the flames. I wouldn't be able to do it on my own, and if I left it, the fire would burn and burn until the end of the universe.

Enough dawdling. I had until sunrise to complete my commission.

I pulled out the flint and held it, measuring its weight in my hand. Then I struck it, tossed the tiny flame onto the wood, and watched as it all caught fire. I grabbed my knife and poised it over my forearm. My tattoos glowed, sensing the magic I was about to perform. I closed my eyes. I thought of the words, an ancient spell in the language of the Order, one I knew perfectly. I knew everything perfectly. I had just never done it before.

I began to chant.

At first the words were only words, but as they spilled out of my mouth they transformed into magic, and I no longer belonged to myself. My voice was no longer my own. It was the voices of the lost, calling forth the Fire of Amkarja. The knife pierced my skin. I wasn't expecting it. My eyes flew open at the jolt of pain. The knife dug deeper. Blood gushed over my arm. No. No. This wasn't right. It was supposed to be a nick, enough to draw a few drops --

Enough of me remained that I was able to yank the knife away and fling blood into the already-golden flames, completing the spell and igniting the fire. Something whispered at the back of my head. A bit of wisdom. A warning. *Don't look.*

I looked.

It wasn't right. I was supposed to see the lost, figures twining and dancing in the gold of the fire. But instead I saw myself, my face twisted and monstrous. The true me, I thought. The face of an assassin.

Fear flooded through my body. My arm burned from where I had lost control of my knife.

"I'm not lost," I said to the fire.

It roared in response, letting off great waves of heat. Forced by the magic, I drifted close to the fire, wanting to be a part of it, to feel the flames wrap around me like a blanket. I vaguely remembered my task. My commission. "Lisim Sarr," I managed to choke out. "Please, I need to find Lisim Sarr."

My face-in-the-fire snarled at me. Lisim Sarr didn't seem so important anymore. Only the fire; the golden sputtering light. I was close enough to touch it. I knelt down in the sand and leaned forward. The smoke tickled my eyes. The flames licked at my face.

The pain was dazzling.

I screamed. The left side of my face felt as if it had been ripped away. I screamed and fell backward and screamed and screamed and when I hit the ground I didn't hit sand, I hit floorboards, rough-hewn, cold, damp. I couldn't see out of my left eye, everything was blurred and indistinct, but out of my right I saw that overhead was a gapped ceiling of the sort they had in the ice-islands.

"Who the hell are you?"

A man's voice. It cut momentarily through the shriek of my pain. I rolled onto my right side. My left side was still burning, the pain moving inside of me now, sliding into my bloodstream. I lifted my head. The man was wrapped in shaggy furs, but he wasn't an ice-islander. He was Empire. He was a Lisirran.

He was Lisim Sarr, my magic whispered.

For a blinding moment, I didn't know what to do. Sarr leaned over me, squinting, and then his eyes went wide, and he recognized me, bleeding and burning though I was, and through my good eye I saw him drawing up his magic.

The Order trained me well, all those years ago, when I

was nothing but a scared little boy. They left me with no choice but to be an assassin in all moments. The pain was paralyzing, but still I conjured up my speed, what little remained of it. In one blurred motion I pulled out my sword and I drew it across Sarr's belly. His blood splattered across the floor, and he died. I didn't feel anything. Everything hurt too much.

I reached out one shaking hand and slapped it into his blood. I didn't trust my own blood; it had betrayed me to the fire. But I used the blood of this wicked man and I fell backward through the shadows, through Kajjil, back over the sea and the ice, back to the Empire.

I WAS IN A BED, soft and luxurious and familiar. I sank into the blankets. I couldn't feel my body; it was like being in Kajjil, but I wasn't in Kajjil. I wasn't at the Order either. This wasn't an Order bed. It smelled of river water and perfume.

"Leila." My voice rasped and came out barely above a whisper.

"Shhh, don't talk." A shadow fell over me. I was aware of a hand stroking my hair but I couldn't feel it.

"I can't feel --"

"Oh, Naji, you never listen. I asked you not to talk." The bed moved beneath me. I turned my head a little. Leila was sitting beside me, her hand stroking my hair. I saw this but didn't feel it.

"You were very stupid," she said.

I didn't answer.

"I told you not to go after him."

Him. Sarr. I'd killed him. Only then did I notice the yellow sunlight in the windows. I'd completed my commission. But I still felt like I was being punished.

I tried to sit up and Leila nudged me back down, gently. "You aren't well. I worked a spell for the pain but I'm afraid it's too strong for you to go wandering around."

"I don't feel myself."

"Well, that's what I had to do to take the pain away." She shrugged. There was something in her expression I couldn't place. Distance or sadness or revulsion. Or maybe all three mixed together. I didn't know what to make of it. I didn't know what to make of any of this. I wondered if the fire was still burning in the desert. It needed to be extinguished.

"Why aren't I at the Order?" I said. "I tried— after everything— I meant to go there."

"I don't know. I woke up last night to your screaming and found you bleeding all over the floor." Her hand dropped away and disappeared from my sight. "You stank of blood magic. And you were --" She stopped.

"What? I was what?"

I kept seeing the fire flickering in my head, golden and sparking, my twisted face in the flames. Not exactly my face, no— my face as it was seen by the people of the Empire. My face as if it belonged to a monster.

I looked at Leila, and she was trying to keep her expression blank and failing.

"What!" I said. "What's wrong with me?"

"Nothing." She sounded insincere.

"Leila!" I struggled on the bed, trying to push myself up. I felt as if I were tied down. "After all this, you're still going to keep secrets from me? Really?"

She narrowed her eyes. "I told you not to go," she said. "I don't call that keeping a secret."

"Leila, what the *hell* is wrong with me?"

She went still. I thrashed on the bed and then exhaustion overpowered me and I went still too. I stared up at the patterns of sunlight on the ceiling. In the empty space where my body should have been I felt creeping, dreadful coldness.

The bed lightened. I dropped my head to the side. Leila was rummaging in the drawer of her vanity. She wore a backless dress and her skin glimmered in the yellow light. It was beautiful.

She walked back over to me and sat down and laid the mirror in her lap.

"What is it?" I whispered.

She hesitated.

"Show me!"

Leila sighed and held up the mirror. It was small, filigreed with little carved flowers. It looked expensive. I noticed all this before I noticed the face. Not my face. The face in the flames. My face, only monstrous.

I didn't understand what I was seeing at first. Then Leila spoke.

"It'll heal, of course, but there will be a scar."

She handed me the mirror and stepped away. My face-that-wasn't-my-face stared back at me. The right side was fine, but the left was melted, the skin reddened and charred. At first I couldn't connect that face to my body. And then I could.

"It's a shame it had to happen by magic," Leila said. "Otherwise there might've been something we could do about it."

I hurled the mirror aside and it shattered on the floor. Leila looked at it with a calm, implacable expression.

"Although you might find something at the night market. To *help*, even if it wouldn't get rid of it completely."

"You don't care," I said.

"What?"

"About helping me."

She fell silent.

"I'm scarred. What would you want with a scarred man? I know you, Leila. You care too much about beautiful things."

She didn't answer, and I knew I was right. I forced myself up to sitting, ignoring her protests. I still couldn't feel my body but I could feel my anger, my humiliation, my sorrow.

"Naji, wait," she said.

"I need to go back." I pushed out of the bed and slammed up against the wall. A narrow strip of shadow stretched out from beside the vanity. I stumbled toward it.

"Don't," Leila said, but I noticed that she didn't bother to stand up, that she didn't otherwise try to stop me.

I didn't look at her as the shadows crawled around me. It was exhausting, stepping into the darkness. But I couldn't look at Leila anymore. I couldn't look at myself.

In those seconds before I arrived back at the Order, my thoughts went to the woman at the dance hall. The smoky blue light. Her spangled dress. I thought of how she had smiled at me. How she hadn't been frightened.

And I knew she would be frightened if she saw me now.

The End.

Acknowledgments

Thanks to Amanda Rutter at Angry Robot for requesting these three stories to accompany *The Assassin's Curse* and *The Pirate's Wish*.

Special thanks to my agent Stacia Decker for suggesting I release these stories on my own, cementing what I'd already been thinking myself.

And finally, thanks to Holly Lyn Walrath for transforming the manuscript into this handy book form.

Read more about Naji, Marjani, and the manticore in *The Magic of Blood and Sea.*

About the Author

Cassandra Rose Clarke's novels have been finalists for the Philip K. Dick Award, *the Romantic Times* Reviewer's Choice Award, and YALSA's Best Fiction for Young Adults. Her poetry has placed second in the Rhysling Awards, been nominated for the Pushcart Prize, and appeared in Strange Horizons, Star*Line, and elsewhere. Her latest novel is *Halo: Battle Born*, forthcoming from Scholastic.

Cassandra graduated in 2006 from The University of St. Thomas with a B.A. in English, and two years later she completed her master's degree in creative writing at The University of Texas at Austin. In 2010 she attended the Clarion West Writer's Workshop in Seattle, where she was a recipient of the Susan C. Petrey Clarion Scholarship Fund. She is currently the associate director for a Houston-based literary arts nonprofit, Writespace.

facebook.com/authorcassandraroseclarke

twitter.com/seeorsea

instagram.com/cassandraroseclarke

About the Cover Artist

Maria Anisimova is a freelance illustrator and concept artist based in Madrid (Spain). Fantasy art is her main passion. When not drawing, she can be found traveling, reading, and petting dogs. Visit her portfolio at behance.net/manisimova.

www.ingramcontent.com/pod-product-compliance
Lightning Source LLC
Chambersburg PA
CBHW050154110726
47898CB00008B/2792